living for the city

living
for the
city

jervey tervalon

Incommunicado Press
P.O.BOX 99090 SAN DIEGO CA 92169 USA

©1998 Incommunicado
Contents © Jervey Tervalon
"Marcella" © Tim Stiles

ISBN 1-888277-08-4
First Printing

Book and cover design by Gary Hustwit
Cover and title page photos by Jervey Tervalon
Author photo by Earl Brown
Edited by Donna Wingate and Gary Hustwit

Printed in the USA

Contents

Foreword

Foreword

I SAW JERVEY TERVALON FOR THE FIRST TIME more than twenty years ago, when he was just eighteen. Jervey was newly enrolled in Marvin Mudrick's writing class, which I had already been taking for a long time. Anyway, I looked him over—he was big, restless, self-conscious, and when he made comments about the stories that were read (Mudrick read our stories out loud), he seemed bright, good-humored, not very articulate. As a human being he seemed to still be in the "promising" stage, all raw material. And if I'd had to guess at what kind of stories he might write, I'd have said that they too would probably be, at best, promising.

The day Jervey's first story was read, I wasn't there. But I know pretty well how it went over.

It was a story called "Godhood's Beginning," and had already won a prize in a Science Fiction contest. Jervey, as he told me recently, was proud of it, and it wasn't unreasonable of him to hope—or even except—that this new teacher might like the story in the same way and for the same reasons that the judges of the contest liked it.

Mudrick's method of teaching was simple. Students, as they came into the room, would put their manuscripts on a table at the front. Mudrick would come in just past the hour, sit down at the table, shuffle through the pile of stories, pick one and, without identifying or naming the author, begin reading aloud. When he'd read as much as he felt was worth reading, he'd stop and either ask for comments or begin making comments himself.

Mudrick read a couple of pages of "Godhead's Beginning," stopped, and said something like, "I don't know why any of you would waste your time writing this kind of drivel. The only excuse for it that I can even imagine, is that you consider your own life to be of no conceivable interest, to you or to anyone else—and I find that hard to believe…"

Jervey, remembering this, laughed and said, "I wasn't sure what 'drivel' meant, but I could tell that it wasn't complimentary. I was stunned, I guess. And it was worse because for some reason I trusted his judgement."

In truth it was kind of a release for him. He went home, or wherever it is that students go, and wrote a few paragraphs about the life he knew: a couple of kids, young boys from South-Central L.A., discover an old woman half-sitting half-lying on the steps in front of a house. Gradually they realize she is dead.

At the next class meeting Mudrick read it aloud and said that, as far as it went, it was good. Jervey went home then and wrote "Flight Control" (pg. 110).

Mudrick read it to the class. I wish I could say that we responded as we should have responded, or even that we were startled into silence. Instead we were dull and tentative, and Mudrick, after hearing a little of what we could think of to say, stopped us, and made some remarks of his own that now seem to me wonderfully prescient.

He said (so far as I can remember) that, "Most of us like to think of art as a kind of struggle. The artist has strong feelings about the world, or about experiences in the world, or imagines or envisions the world in some new way—and then, afterward, has to work hard to find a fitting means of expression, a form, or whatever you want to call it.

"What it's like to be that kind of artist is fairly easy for the rest of us to imagine: we see our own minds as working in more or less the same way, even if they don't work as well.

"But there's also another kind of artist, who makes art without any apparent struggle at all. Even this kind of artist has to learn, of course. Even someone like Mozart can be seen learning—from his father, his older sister, from other musicians and composers, from scores that he reads, music that he hears. But he learns so quickly, and with so little conscious effort, that most of us can't imagine—can't even have the *illusion* of imagining—what it might be like to have a mind of that kind, or what it might feel like to make art in that way.

"But one thing we can do, can even *learn* to do, is to take delight in this kind of art when we come across it—and to recognize this kind of ease of expression when we see it, or hear it."

Mudrick went back through the story, then, rereading almost all of it, but stopping along the way to make comments. At some point he said that in talking about art it's almost impossible not to lapse into abstraction. "For example, we could say, 'Yes, this story is about the way attractive, comfortable, well-established friendships can be disrupted and even endangered by love,' and this would be true. But to say it is to miss about ninety-nine percent of what affects us, affects me at least, when it's being read.

"The details of the story are so *exact*. The author's sense of comic time is right—just right…and you get the impression, and of course it's a false impression, an illusion, that the author is saying virtually nothing at all in his own voice, and that he is never tempted to interfere with the actions of his characters, that he doesn't *arrange* anything, that he doesn't intrude on what these characters, in this situation, would naturally say. And yet you know that he has arranged it all, because it happens so quickly. In life, the situation would take all afternoon to develop, and its energy would dissipate itself into a thousand irrelevant directions. Here, it is beautifully compressed, and gains the kind of force that art always does gain from compression. But it is all done with so little effort, with no apparent effort at all…and I know some of you think that apparent effort is a good thing. But it's not! In art it's not. In art and love."

Something like that is a small part of what Mudrick said. I hope that the people who were there will forgive me for getting it partly wrong.

Jervey's reaction to such praise? I don't know how it made

him feel, but it affected his work in the best possible way. That is to say, it had no obvious effect at all. The stories he went on producing for Mudrick's class—handing in a new one every couple of weeks—continued to be just as calm, lucid, touching, funny, and sure-footed. Several of them are collected here, virtually unchanged, under the subtitle *Local Color*.

The stories that Tervalon has written more recently, and which are collected here under the subtitle *Knucklehead*, have all the good qualities that the earlier stories have. In addition to this, though, these later stories contain the humane and reflective intelligence of a grown-up. Tervalon has a past now; he has thought about that past well, and has learned how to fit the world of his childhood into the larger world.

One last note: It's interesting that the dedication of Tervalon's first published book, *Understand This*, reads: "To the memory of Marvin Mudrick."

    – Max Schott

This book is dedicated to Gina and Giselle.

marcella

Had new clothes on
the last time
because her lip had seams
and her eyelids were painted shut.

And the Reverend sang
the sisters
out their seats
loud as Hell amen
but nobody woke.

Then they wept
like they knew her
and watched her grow up
from skinny pimples and smile
amen.

There were two bullets
in her head
and they never let on;
but she would never
comb her hair like that.

And then we lined up
to give the last look so
I craved cherry jolly ranchers
stuck in them big pickles
like every day after school
in ninth grade.

And when she giggled at me and said
to shave my armpits
if they itched
even if I was a boy.

– Tim Stiles

living for the city

Part One: Knucklehead

The Sixties

I MUST HAVE BEEN A HAPPY LITTLE four-year-old boy to see him after all those months, but I don't remember that. What I do remember is night in Texas, blanket-like black sky shot through with flecks of white, and a road, a ribbon running into the black horizon, and the occasional glinting red or green eyes of deer poised on the edge of the highway, scaring me so bad he talked about it for years. How I trembled so hard I got him scared, tried to get closer and closer, rooting a space under his arm, that's how scared I was. Daddy knew it. He sang "Deep in the Heart of Texas," as though that gigantic state—blacker than any closet I ever managed to lock myself in—could have a heart.

Mama says it was Daddy's idea to move out West. Did she want to? Was it an idea which appealed to her? Or did Daddy at that time have power over her? The mountains, that's what he told me, not like the flat land of Louisiana where you could see the sky curve into the sea, but I didn't believe that. Daddy was a creature of the same-old same-old. A chance? Taking a gamble because he liked the mountains didn't sound like my Daddy. What he did do is buy his brother's house in a neighborhood ripe and ready to slide into decline. Mama also said it was his idea to leave me in New Orleans with my Grumma while the rest of the family moved out to California.

And even though I was very young, I vividly remember the panic I felt when I realized I would be left alone there, a four-year-old boy frightened of my Grumma's cramped, dark and cluttered, but very clean shotgun house and of her relentless prayers all through the evening. I loved my Grumma, but she was so old. I was afraid she might die and I'd be left alone in that quiet, little house with the ghosts I knew to be there. At night I listened to her mumbling the rosary, wondering if she'd keep on breathing long enough for Daddy to come and get me like he said he would. After a few nights I decided to run away. Maybe I thought I could find them or maybe I was hoping for Daddy to magically appear and find me. Somehow I ended up under Grumma's house, in the dusty crawl space. Grumma called my name but I ignored her, even when I heard the anger in her voice turn to anxiety. Night fell. I watched the neighbors walking about, looking for me with their flashlights, calling for me as they searched the neighborhood. Finally a blinding flashlight shone into my hiding place, and a deep voiced, "Here he is," startled me. A big man grabbed my arm and lifted me out of there and brought me to the porch. Grumma flung the screen door open and hugged me. She thanked the man and carried me into the house. But soon as she did, she sat before her shrine, a low chest of drawers with pictures of Christ and statues of the saints, and her rosary hanging from the side of a mirror. She took down the rosary, and began to cry.

"Why'd you hide from me? You almost broke my heart."

"I wasn't hiding from you, Grumma. I was just hiding."

I felt guilty watching her cry, wondering if I would try to run away again but I didn't have time to plan another escape. Daddy finally arrived to take me to our new home in Los Angeles.

All Along the Watchtower

WE KNEW THE NEIGHBORHOOD WAS CHANGING. We being the knuckleheads, Gumbo, Onla and me, but the fellas had no idea. They didn't seem to notice how much fear was on the streets. Somehow their age blinded them to all the teenagers with vicious sneers in bright blue or green bomber jackets, wearing jeans starched and ironed at home, shiny with dirt. That ass kicking I received trying to visit the wrong-number girl woke me up to what was happening around the avenues and all through black L.A. Suddenly, our neighborhoods were divided up into territories with hard and fast boundaries which, if you crossed them could result in a serious beating, even get you killed. But it didn't affect the fellas. As though sitting under the big tree, with their nice cars and dope to be smoked, excluded them from our world. Even in '72, when the drive-bys started and we took to squatting behind whatever was solid if a car slowed as it passed down the street, the fellas just didn't seem to notice how jumpy and unhappy we were with the turn of events. Then a rash of shootings swept through the neighborhood. Dinky got shot at a party, a glancing blow which broke his arm and gave him something to brag about. But it was one of those events which shaped the future. Not that I liked going to house parties, dark living rooms filled with teenagers, booming music, spiked punch and off-brand potato chips. Half of us hugging the walls to get up the courage to ask someone to dance, and the other half on the dance floor working up a sweat. But then some guys couldn't afford new tailor-made knit shirts, or shiny, blunt biscuits, those ugly, thick shoes. Or they had short hair, couldn't grow a huge afro like the Jacksons. Maybe they couldn't accept the humiliation most of us knuckleheads had to go through at those parties. The girls were not interested in dancing with junior high school freshmen. They didn't want to dance with geeks wearing thousand-eyes shoes. So we were ignored, and that was fine with me. I was willing to hold up a wall until I understood the intricacies of the Texas hop/cha-cha, but I never got a chance, parties lost all interest for most of us knuckleheads. Up at the Mack family house, at their weekly party, I stood next to Onla, both of us in our stiff church clothes looking proper and dumb, instead of cool and dangerous. Carol, a girl in our class who we tried to avoid because she was fat like a sumo, was eyeing us. Tonight she had on a flouncy dress which made her look like a huge, roving sunflower, trying to find someone to dance with to the "Psychedelic Shack." She grabbed Onla's skinny arm, and said, "Let's go," and he threw himself in reverse, went down to the ground and dug in his heels, leverage to break her hold, then he latched onto me.

"Dance with him," he said.

She nodded, put her arm around my waist and with that grip pulled me from the wall. She had me but I wasn't going to dance. I didn't have to. All our attention turned to the ruckus at the door. Somebody didn't want to pay the 25 cents.

"Turning this shit out!" I heard someone shout.

BOOM!!

I have never heard something so loud; shattered plaster rained down on us. The record player fell over and exploded onto the floor. It was totally dark because the red light got blown away with the ceiling. We were down on all fours, as was everyone, feeling our way forward—but which way was out?

"See, ya'll got your shit turned out!"

The room was strangely quiet as though we were at church. Finally, when it seemed as if the party crashers had gone, crying started. People were standing up, rushing out onto the porch and the lawn. The room had emptied except for me and a few other people. Carol was there in a corner, blubbering. Onla was gone, just like him to make a getaway. I went outside, dodging the angry knots of Mack relatives. A gang unto themselves, planning revenge. Nobody seemed hurt. Those who weren't related to the Macks or tied to them out of friendship had moved down the street, making themselves distant targets.

I walked the block home passing people; nobody noticed me, as if the shooting blinded everyone to everything else. Most of my part of the block were on Kay Kay and Trice's porch: Onla and Kay Kay, Trice and her new boyfriend, Roachie, and retarded Sally. Usually, when Sally was around, Onla and me and most of us under 16 and shorter than 5'8 kept our distance. She was hell on us young guys, tossing us around and stealing our money if she felt like it, and she often felt like it.

"Garvy looks scared! Bet you peed on yourself."

I didn't say anything, that was the smart thing.

Though she was our age, Sally had quickly matured into a rock-hard, deep-voiced, cartoon-like bully who would have provoked a lot of nightmares if she were a guy, but being a girl…a girl with lots of desires, she made us sweat in a number of complex ways.

"You was inside?" Trice asked.

Trice and Roachie didn't go to the party because Roachie's family didn't get along with the Macks.

"Yeah, I was inside, me and Onla."

"Bet you was scared," Roachie said.

It was amazing how big his afro was, so huge it flopped down to his shoulders.

"Yeah, I was scared but Onla beat me out by a long shot."

"Yeah?" Roachie said, and everybody turned to look at Onla. Onla smiled nervously and folded his arms around himself.

"Onla's always been scary. He probably pooted on himself," Sally said.

"It was them William boys from Hillcrest, that was what they were saying," Onla said.

Roachie laughed.

"It wasn't nobody from Hillcrest. It was them Harlem Cribs. They turned it out."

Roachie nodded as if to affirm his statement and everybody nodded along with him.

That name again: Cribs. The name was circling through the neighborhood faster and faster. The Mack family and the William family were bad enough; they got into serious stuff. We also had the Brotherhood, a motorcycle club with big weightlifting men, but they were peaceable, at least to the neighborhood. The Cribs were different. They were us, regular brothers transformed into gangsters. Even their name implied they were homeboys—they were from the crib. Suddenly, out of nowhere came organization. Not any kind of organization, not one built on mutually shared goals and a leadership hierarchy. It wasn't like on TV and those old gangs from New York where members had titles such as Minister of Information or Sergeant of Arms. No, the Cribs were a home-grown Barbarian Horde which appeared on the block one hot summer day in their sporty outfits of Bomber jackets with thick fur collars, Levi's shiny with starched dirt, black croaker sac shoes and a black or red handkerchief, starched rigid. They came, sprung up from the concrete, the lawns, the backyards and especially the schools and they ruled. At first nobody belonged to the Cribs, but many kids had a big brother in their ranks. (Mysteriously the "b" became a "p" and they became known as the Crips.) The ultimate threat started to circulate: "Fool, let me drop a dime and I'll get your house knee-deep in lowriders."

That was something to really fear, the idea of your enemy having your house surrounded with Crips in lowriders, hydraulics bouncing the Impalas like rubber balls. Then, like in *Night of the Body Snatchers*, kids started converting; some big head pootbutt with bad teeth and breath got the "look," and the attitude, that whole sullen maniac trip, slit-eyed, laconic, barely even a nod and then on a bad day, "What fool?! Yeah niggah, this is Crip here."

Of course every now and then they would have to rat pack someone just to show the world how it was done, but that escalated quickly into its more deadly variant—the stomp. That's how Lamar died, stomped flat at a house party. Cool, handsome Lamar. It wasn't a mystery why he was stomped, all over the city, throughout black L.A., it was happening, a kind of teenage arms race. While in our part of the world it was the Crips, a mile south it was the Brims, east the Pirus, and all of them with as much of an intolerant view of outsiders as the Crips. So Lamar, the handsome young ladies' man with no intention of beating on anyone, was killed by a bunch of fools who kicked him in the head till he stopped breathing, because he was too good looking and he might have stolen one of the girls they didn't have in the first place. His stomping made obvious what everybody knew was happening: our blocks, which were like small, self-contained towns, were now territories to be defended as though the avenues and streets had natural resources or religious significance. Notions of self defense, of preemptive strikes, the need to never be caught slipping, became a way of life. It was inevitable, or so it seemed, that sooner or later we all were going to die some stupid, embarrassing death.

All those outdoor gatherings, something one would expect in Southern California, an afternoon with family and friends in one of the many neighborhood parks, became a big gamble. Like the Festival in Black, where some good-hearted community people who believed in black pride and the need for black businesses and who gave crafts-people and t-shirt vendors and incense sellers an opportunity to make some money; those kinds of events were dying out fast. But then it was exciting to see all the families having picnic lunches or barbecuing and all those fine girls who would never talk to us and the hip people, the people who put the festival on. It was easy to tell them because they wore cool black t-shirts with "Festival In Black" in flowing cursive script and a line drawing of a black man and woman in a sort of heroic style, huge afros and big muscles on the guy, big breasts on the girl. But these events that brought the community together became unpopular. Who wanted to be out in the open, exposed to whatever might jump off, now that teenagers ruled the streets, unafraid of dying and unafraid of killing somebody.

For some reason Sidney, Winnie and Jude let me and Onla trip with them to the festival. They were sitting down under a tree near the bandstand where the music groups were playing, smoking joints and drinking beers, cooling out. Onla and I went on another hot dog run; it was boring watching them get loaded, because we didn't. We wandered around counting our change, spying on the girls, looking at all the cool African stuff in the booths, not paying attention to, but hearing the music, drums and horns, saxophones...something happening in the distance up where it was most crowded by the bandstand. We could see the drummers in their African outfits moving around on the stage and people in front of the stage struggling, rolling on the grass and then other picnickers chain-reacting, grabbing their stuff and running for high ground. Me and Onla did what we had grown accustomed to do. Instead of the habit we had for years, of running towards trouble to see what we could see and what tales we could carry back to our neighborhood, now we high-tailed it, wise enough to know we couldn't stand at the edge of trouble and expect to avoid it. Nowadays the fists and bullets flew in all directions.

We ran back to Jude and Winnie, ready to get to the car and get the hell out of there, but they weren't on the knoll near the trees and basketball courts.

"Where are they?" I asked, but Onla didn't bother to answer.

From the knoll we could see the trouble spreading; the knot of fighting had swelled to a mob and more and more people were running from it in various directions. Some had even caught up to us and passed us on their way to the parking lot.

Then the hollow, dumb sounds of gunshots, and the screams and even more people running. And Onla, cool calm Onla, started to panic.

"Fuck! We gotta get out of here."

"Yeah," I said. "Where are we gonna go? We got to be ten miles from the Aves."

"So?" he said, and started pogo-ing up down.

"What you doing?"

"Seeing which way to go."

Things were getting scary. If Onla did something dumb and tried to run home, I'd have to try to hang with him. He knew the way and I had no idea what direction home was in. More shots in the distance, more people rushing up, a big woman shoved Onla aside so hard he almost fell.

"They wouldn't just drive off and leave us."

I was sure they wouldn't do anything that dumb.

Mama would probably throw high and inside on Winston with the frying pan this time, instead of low and out. I was sure even if Onla wasn't, that they had to be somewhere near. I trotted away to the parking lot as it was starting to clear out. There was a big jam-up at the exit. There, near a tree was Winston's Jag. We just hadn't seen it, but there they were. We ran for it, right ahead of the biggest wave of people. Jude was in the back seat, Sidney and Winston were in the front with the windows rolled up to keep the contact in. Jude had his window down. Onla dived right in, feet barely clearing Jude's head.

"What the fuck is wrong with you?" Jude shouted.

Onla unlocked the door for me and I tried to get in but Onla slipped around me. He didn't want to sit next to Jude and maybe get thrown out.

"You guys should go," I said, trying to be cool cause I knew if I sounded pushy they'd ignore me.

"Man, don't ya'll see! Look!" Onla said.

The gangbangers had arrived, running for their cars and whatever weapons they had stashed in them. Four bloodied and bruised guys got to a lowrider and the trunk opened, out came a shotgun and a handgun. The armed ones led the way back to the park. Onla had scrunched down to the floor in a little heaving ball. I wanted to join him but I was too big to fit. Jude continued sipping his beer and the joint continued circulating between the three of them.

Boom Boom! Pop Pop!

The gangbangers had unloaded at a distance and were running back to the car to reload. They were more than a dozen yards away and their enemies were coming after them.

"Getting pretty wild around here," Sidney said.

"Young knuckleheads," Jude said.

"Let's get out of here!" I said, cause one of the rival gangbangers had stopped on a knoll and let off at the gangbangers near us.

"Go!" Onla shouted.

Jude reached across me and hit Onla in the shoulder so hard his head ricocheted off of the car window.

"You guys shut up. Nobody's worried about us. Running away might get 'em thinking."

"What?" I said.

Winnie was good and buzzed, pointing to four squad cars coming down on Manchester.

"Man, fucking pigs!" Sidney said.

"Yeah," Winnie said, "We gotta go!"

Winston stepped into action, gone was his beer and weed-induced stupor. He wheeled the car around and ignored the congested exit. He drove the Jag across the parking lot, across the sidewalk and over the edge of the curb. The heavy front end of the sedan boomed down onto the street, then the rear wheels landed, and we bounced about again.

"Damn," Winnie said, "I gotta replace those shocks."

He cut across two lanes and turned along with the police. At first I had no idea what he was trying to do, maybe get us all arrested. But then I saw more police cars coming down the street we just turned off. We arrived there just as the police were getting ready to block the intersections with squad cars. Winston waved to them as though he knew them. For a moment it seemed as though the policemen were going to pull us over and get a whiff of Winston's weed and beer-scented breath. Winston though, had risen to the occasion. He gave that million-dollar, matchbook smile, and his straight teeth and green eyes and his white skin reassured the cop, convinced him that the Jag with the longhaired white guy and his black friends (and not even that black) wasn't really worth stopping. We drove away, back to the quieter Westside.

It continued on like that, us knuckleheads seeing our world undergoing blurring change, and the fellas seemingly missing out on the whole thing as if they were walking on different sidewalks, breathing another kind of air.

Maybe it was because they had money, enough income so they weren't forced to hang out in the neighborhood. They didn't hang out at the Baldwin Theater every weekend cause it was the neighborhood theater. They had cars to drive to the Marina or Westwood.

A few years back the Baldwin Theater was hip to hang out at, check out the double feature, *Hang 'em High* and *Where Eagles Dare*. Maybe some of them cool Hammer horror films. Then the black exploitation flicks were really live: *Coffee T.N.T., Foxy Brown, Nigger Charlie, Abbey the Black Exorcist*. And young love was there too, couples huddled up while the nons like me and Gumbo who couldn't pull females had to content ourselves with hot dogs and popcorn. Man, you couldn't keep us out of there.

But it got to be a dicey thing wanting to go to the Baldwin, and getting home became another worry altogether. Of course it was the boys in gang-bang blue packing the restrooms. That was another manifestation of the new neighborhood order. I wouldn't drink sodas no matter how thirsty I got from salty popcorn. No way I wanted to go in the restroom and be surrounded by gangbangers, and if you didn't know a few of them it could get serious. Somebody might ask, "Hey, homes, loan me a dollar," and that was the worst thing about it, it wasn't a standard kind of jack where you could come out with a quarter, give it up and slip away. These chumps were raising the rate to a point where the average pootbutt couldn't stand it. There would go the hot dog, the bus ride, even the phone call home. You'd have to get bold and say, "Sorry, man, I ain't got it," then there would be that long moment where everyone is looking at you. Encircled by his partners, your accuser ups the ante.

"Stand for a search?"

Me, I'd try pulling my pockets inside out. "See," I'd say, and walk my ass out of the restroom. Sometimes though, we'd see some knucklehead standing there on that nasty restroom floor, socks in hand, barefoot. He had to undergo a full search.

The bus ride home got to be crazy too, buses seemed to make gangsters nuts. Once, after the movie theater closed and everybody hit the bus stop at the same time, the bus pulled up and stopped like a rookie bus driver would, not like those bus drivers who knew the ropes, who would speed by and avoid what they knew would be nothing but trouble. Gumbo and me got on because Gumbo hated walking. We were towards the front of the crush of passengers, and got to board first. We sat close to the bus driver in our silent hope that we would be safe. And like clockwork, the first paying gangbanger slipped to the rear door and forced it open. Then the flood gates opened. The mob by the back door flowed in filling the rear of the bus first. An old man and woman sat frightened behind the rear door well. There wasn't anything for them to do but huddle together, faces tight with worry and shock, and hope to weather the wave of teenagers.

That day we both knew this bus driver had lost control of the bus. We needed to get off before it got really insane. I waited for Gumbo to make the move. He was wider than me, it would be easier to follow in his substantial wake. But he wasn't having any of that. I was older and taller, a fifteen year old with some facial hair, it was expected of me to lead. I stood up and immediately my seat was taken by a guy in a Bomber jacket with a fake fur collar, fur so white I knew he had just gotten it, same with his blue beanie, right off the rack; he was exulting in his new uniform.

I put my head down and got by the panicked bus driver who knew he had lost it. Control was in the hands of a teenage mob and they wanted his transfers.

"Get off" he shouted.

Nobody but me and Gumbo heard or paid attention to him, we shoved our way down the stairwell and through the crowd still trying to board. Finally, free of people pushing against us, we turned to see the bus driver fleeing the bus, broken-field running down La Brea.

We started walking because we had no choice. Even as kids it seemed weird to have to walk somewhere. It used to be easier to just beg parents for a ride, but now as a teenager that was no longer a possibility. How would that look going over to some girl's house in my Daddy's beat up Galaxie 500? So we walked home from the Baldwin because it was safer than taking the bus, but also because it was an adventure slipping by the Jungle, walking on the edge of the street, listening for voices and if hearing them, retreating down another block or even diving behind hedges to wait for the hoodlums to troop by. Sometimes though, it would be so quiet and empty walking down Coliseum in that affluent area, that we walked in the center of the street like it was our own personal road.

Once we got away from the sprawling clusters of apartments in the Jungle where we had to be quiet and watchful, we could talk loudly in the neighborhoods which were still mostly Japanese with their clover lawns and their decorative pagodas, and then the black affluent neighborhood near Audubon Junior High. The homes were beautiful, nicer than what we would see on TV. Beautiful two-story Spanish homes, with large windows and ornate wrought-iron fences to keep the riffraff out.

THEN I GOT A JOB, not another half-assed, washing the neighbor's car or cutting lawns and having to try to sneak out our lawn mower without Mama finding out. She usually did and she'd yell at me for using things I can't replace.

No, it was a real job tutoring little kids in a science program out of the community center at USC, $1.95 an hour, more than $10.00 a day, great money for a fifteen year old.

The guy who hired me was a serious black man who just graduated with a degree in biology from Berkeley. His name was Ron and right off I knew he was different from the fellas on the Ave. Sure some of the fellas were serious; Walter was as serious as a walking heart attack about money as was Sidney, but skinny, dark-skinned, well-spoken Ron wasn't in it for the cash. Ron was really smart but that didn't set him apart. Jude was smart too, if you got him to talk about missiles and tanks and warfare. Winnie was a gifted mechanic and was great with numbers but neither he nor Jude seemed interested in anything beyond smoking weed, playing basketball and going to work. Ron was a different kind of bird.

He received a grant to run a science program for minority kids out of USC's community center. I knew Ron from Foshay where he ran the science program after school. He heard that I won a science fair with a model rocket I built.

"The job's yours," he said. "Just get your work permit. Fill out this form and I'll submit it for you."

I guess he saw some leadership potential in me but I think he was probably asking everybody and whoever turned in the application first would get the job. I filled out mine and forged my Mama's signature and returned it in minutes.

"You must really want this job. You'll like helping little brothers and sisters learn the importance of science."

I nodded, but I wonder if he knew that I knew more about science fiction than actual science. We started the program soon as summer break began, me and a dozen other black and brown kids stepping onto the grounds of USC for the first time, a spot of color on that very white campus.

Most of the kids I was supposed to tutor were seventh grade scrubs from Foshay. Professors would invite us into the labs inside an old ivy-covered building with gargoyles above the entrance to give us tours and a little lecture. "Water is made up of two molecules of hydrogen, one of oxygen," I was told on more than one tour.

Afterward, we'd head back to the community center with kids asking me questions I couldn't answer.

"Why can't you see them molecules?" some big headed kid asked me.

"Cause they're too small. Don't you remember what the professor said?"

"But you can see them. I see water all the time." The kid pointed to the water faucet and I wondered why this kid was asking me.

"We don't fall off the earth because gravity is pulling us down!"

"I don't see nothing holding me down," another kid said.

"Cause it's like a magnet."

"I don't see no magnet holding me down."

That's when I just would shrug and walk away, more aware of how I didn't know much more than the scrubs I looked down on.

Ron was very excited about the program. He'd give us little speeches about the importance of what we were doing.

"We can't make it as a people if we don't have the engineers or the scientists. Not all of us are going to be athletes or entertainers. You all have a much better chance being a brain surgeon than a quarterback for the Rams."

The kids seemed shocked; they thought if they stayed out of trouble and stayed in school, a professional career in sports was a lock. Billy, one of the tough seventh graders was sure going to make it at football even though he was the runt of the group.

Ron did get most of us to learn how to solve a simple problem with a slide rule and how to use a microscope and even how to do some math, but I think what everybody really liked about the program were the weekly field trips.

"Where to this week?" a kid would ask.

"Griffith Park Observatory," Ron would say dryly because he knew what was coming next, the plea for thrills.

"Man, what about Disneyland? They got robots and Tomorrowland."

"Y'all shut up and learn to work those slide rules. Then we'll go."

We never went because we could never work the slide rules as well as Ron wanted us to. That was okay. Most of us had been to Disneyland. Where Ron took us we had never heard of but it was usually interesting. Once we went to a naval base in San Diego and got to see docked submarines. We actually were there to check out the tide pools near the base but Ron got interested in the subs, and we couldn't get near enough to make him happy because of the fifteen-foot-high fence with concertina wire at the top and posted warnings, "No Trespassers!"

We hiked up the sand dunes to the highway where we could see the submarines more clearly—giant black tubes with crossed wings.

"One of those things cost half a billion dollars," Ron said angrily.

"How much is that?"

"More than a million?" someone else asked.

"No, it ain't," the first kid replied.

"One of those subs could blow the whole world up," Ron said as though it really depressed him. I didn't believe him.

"Not the whole world," I said.

"Maybe L.A.?" a kid asked.

Ron's sisters, Penny and Terry, two girls around our age looked pained as Ron explained about nuclear missiles.

"He oughta be a preacher," Penny, the older of the two, said.

"I knew I should have stayed home, but mama said I had to go with you," Terry said.

"I didn't want to go. Ron said I had to go," Penny replied.

Both of them fixed on me, finally noticing that I wasn't paying attention to the seventh graders as I was supposed to do.

"Don't you hate having to go to all these boring places?" Penny asked, in a clear, correct voice that most of us at Foshay thought of as being white. I tried to conceal my happiness at having one of these pretty middle-class girls talking to me, but I liked going to labs and tide pools and museums. It was like being in a science fiction movie.

"Yeah, it's boring," I said, looking disgusted.

"Stop lying," Terry said, "you know you like all this science stuff."

"You leave him alone. You know you like him," Penny said.

"He's too young for me. He's your speed."

Ron had finished explaining the perils of nuclear warfare to the captive band of seventh graders.

"I should see if we can go on a tour of one of these bad boys. Let ya'll get close to the missiles that could end the world as we know it," Ron said.

The seventh graders began to peel off one by one, slipping away to the school bus. But nuclear war scared me even if no one else seemed interested. I hated the first Friday of each month because the air raid sirens would sound, and sometimes I'd think it was the last Friday or another day and that the world was gonna blow up before I grew pubic hair.

"Shadows, after they dropped the bomb on Hiroshima all that was left of some people was a shadow outline, just ashes on the ground, they were fried so fast," Ron said shaking his head.

"Man," I said, knowing that I had another image of the bomb along with huge mushroom clouds and gigantic ants.

"Only twenty minutes away from a missile fired in Siberia and we're all dead before we know it."

I stood there thinking about how I'd go, on the toilet, cutting the lawn, picking up the dog mess in the backyard. I wished the bombs would wait until I had a girlfriend.

"Come on, Garv," he said shaking me out of my morbid funk. "We've got to go. I've scared you enough. That's enough fun for today."

I knew Ron kind of got a kick out of telling us of these end-of-the-world nightmares because I think he knew how dangerous life was in the here and now. Science fiction violence and death was almost a relief from what could happen walking to the liquor store or working at the community center with guys who didn't care for science or science fiction death.

First, it was the little things; all the supplies in Ron's office disappeared. He suspected that someone from the staff of the community center was up to it. How else would they have keys? That was the problem about the community center; the two dozen kids from the science program, plus Ron and me and his sisters had to share a small building with people who didn't seem to do anything but argue and play basketball and be paid for it. We were instructed by Ron to avoid them, "USC got them here on salary so they don't set the school on fire. They know they sold out so they make trouble," Ron said.

The rumors were that Crow, this muscle-bound, tight pants-wearing guy who was the assistant supervisor of the sports program, thought Ron carried himself too highly, and he might have to knock him out. But as disturbing as this rumor was at that moment, I didn't have time to worry about him because the community center became a tensely-armed camp. Crips from my neighborhood were driving through the parking lot flashing hand signs. I was afraid of the Crips but I knew they wouldn't bother to shoot at me and waste a bullet. I wasn't worth it. But I didn't want the community center rabble to know I lived in a Crip neighborhood. That could be serious as a heart attack. Being from somewhere had gotten to be a big point of contention with gangsters, and we were all from someplace if we liked it or not. Being from the Thirties implied that I knew those gangsters on those particular streets and were on reasonably good terms with them. So, it was good to be vague, or even to lie about your address because it was too complicated and dangerous to be honest.

After the flashing of the signs I knew something was going

to happen. These guys had to shoot at those guys and those guys would be back at the community center to shoot at these guys and maybe even me.

"Shouldn't brought his ass up here if he didn't want it kicked," one of the Gladiators said, the gang that most of the community center workers seemed to belong to.

"I don't care if he don't gang-bang. His brother do. Think cause he's some punk-ass lover he won't get beat down."

"Shoulda thought about who runs things up here," another gangster said.

So it was going to happen, a time bomb ticking that could take any of us out. Wayne, another undercover Avenue guy I went to Foshay with, had a job coaching baseball. He was worried too.

"We're straight in the middle of this shit."

"Think something's gonna happen?" I asked.

"Oh, hell yeah. And I'm damn sure gonna lock myself in that bathroom and let these fools kill each other," Wayne said.

That sounded like a good plan so when I wasn't working with the kids I started hanging near to Wayne, looking for that clue to break for the bathrooms. I knew the score from Foshay: run somewhere and lock yourself in till the shooting or the ass kicking stops.

Most of the Gladiators and their sympathizers were ready for whatever might jump off. Enough of them were deep into the martial arts, practicing kicks and punches and coming up with odd weapons I'd never seen before, chains hooked to sickles, short sticks with handles, and one guy even had a samurai sword. I heard they were training with this Korean master, but I wondered if the Korean master guy knew he was dealing with gangsters?

Wayne and I glanced at them as we did our grunt work, sweeping the large main floor of the center.

"Those fools better have something more in their trunks other than that Bruce Lee shit or they gonna get blasted," Wayne said, and I agreed.

Guns ruled the land and they didn't seem to have any. Maybe they knew magic along with the marital arts and could make guns useless, the kind of thing we saw in those Kung Fu movies.

When it happened, it was straight out of the *Wild Bunch*. I was sweeping when I saw shadows stretching across the hard wooden floors of the community center, and one of those shadows had something long and pointed extending from an arm. I should have run but I didn't. I was stuck there in that moment, seeing more gangsters with guns drawn backing up the lead guy.

The Gladiators vanished like ghosts, somehow leaving the center without making a sound or being seen. I would have done the same thing if I saw the Crips coming. Only Crow and Ron were left between the Crips and the community center. Then Crow gave up on trying to look hard enough to stare down six armed men and he broke, zig-zagging for the kitchen. After hesitating for a minute the Crips flowed through the double doors calling out the Gladiators, "Fuck all you punk ass Gladiators!" one of them said.

"We better raise," Wayne said, and we hurriedly walked to the bathrooms but we knew better than to run. The bathroom doors were all locked. We heard voices, girls crying and guys telling them to shut up. So that's where the Gladiators hid. I bet Crow was in there too. Then we heard Ron's voice. First it seemed like he was trying to block their way but then his voice rose. What was he going to do, preach to them?

"Hey, brothers! Calm yourselves. There is no reason for this kind of ugliness."

"What the fuck you know!" the one with the long gun said. He looked familiar, then I realized that it was Dennis, the wannabe gangster who took my bus money a number of times at Foshay. Some people said he had moved up, now supposedly he was the Godfather of the Harlem Crips.

"The guys you're looking for took off when they saw you coming. The rest of the people here are in the science program and none of them gang-bang."

"Stop lying!" Dennis shouted.

"Black man to black man I'm telling you the truth. All the people you want ran off!"

A long pause and then Dennis and his boys started backing off.

I started sweeping again glad to have something to do. Wayne had managed to slip away so it was just Ron and me in the big bare hall and a half dozen Crips with their guns drawn. But now they were no longer faceless thugs. I could see beyond the bomber jackets and croaker sac shoes and the guns, if I didn't know their names I knew their faces. Then Dennis and his boys backed out of the community center, "Tell them Gladiators we're gonna be back!" It wasn't over. I can hear them on the outside of the double doors arguing.

"Fuck 'em! They're hiding. Let's shoot it up."

"Man, let's go," I heard Dennis say.

The arguing continued and poor Ron sagged against a wall as if he knew he had more convincing to do. But Ron didn't wait for them to rush in again guns blasting. He stepped outside.

"Brothers, I understand that you're angry that somebody did you wrong, but there are kids here, that's all."

"Let me check it out," Dennis asked, and before Ron could reply the first guy with the gun craned his head around the door, giving Ron a little respect by not coming back inside. Dennis looked dead at me. I nodded agreeably.

"See any of them Gladiator fools?"

"They ran," is all I managed to say.

"Your pootbutt ass better not be lying."

"I ain't lying," I said, shrugging.

He waved me off and I saw them head out for the parking lot. Ron quickly pulled the doors, but not before we heard a few quick shots causing us all to flatten. After five minutes of quiet, the doors to the bathrooms opened and most kids took off, but the Gladiators were talking about payback. Ron watched looking bone tired. Then he gestured for me to follow him into his office.

"Why do I have to deal with these goddamn idiots?!" he said, sitting heavily at his desk and putting his head down into his hands. Even long after the girls and kids and the Gladiators ventured from the restrooms, Ron sat with his head on the desk. Finally, he looked up at me.

"Go home, and tell all the kids to go before those idiots come back."

I didn't have to tell anybody because we were all cutting out. As I crossed the parking lot making sure to walk between cars in case I needed cover, Wayne appeared, smiling sheepishly.

"Man, we lucked out. We coulda got blasted."

"Yeah, I was scared. I don't know about coming to work tomorrow."

Wayne laughed, "I'm quitting. It's gonna get wicked. The money ain't enough."

Wayne quitting got me to thinking. I decided to take a day off.

THE NEXT MORNING I CALLED RON and told him I was sick. He said he understood and I'd still get paid.

The following morning I caught the bus to USC and I noticed that the front of the community center was pockmarked with bullet holes. It was an interesting thing to see, just like in the movies. The holes made ribbon-like patterns across the face of the building, even smashing a few of the raised letters of the University of Southern California. The Crips had returned and left serious graffiti to let everybody know.

Ron was in the office looking tired and pissed off.

"The police are coming to talk to us about what happened here last night."

"I guess it didn't stop after we went home."

"No, it didn't. I'm sure they all came back here to prove their manhood," Ron said, smirking. "Watch, USC is going to shut the center down because of this."

"Think there's gonna be more trouble?"

"These brothers have a disease that's spreading. They're robots programmed to kill each other."

"You mean like robots with diseases?" I asked. Ron made everything sound like science fiction but he ignored my question.

"Yeah, Garvy. You might want to quit. I can't guarantee your safety. I don't feel safe. I don't want my sisters coming up here."

"I don't mind, I mean it's crazy around here but it's crazy everywhere."

Ron frowned as though whatever he was thinking filled him with disgust.

"You'd think USC would cut us some slack. They know this center is a pit. They just want this nonsense to continue so they can run all the programs off. They act like teaching science is just the same as shooting baskets."

THE POLICE SHOWED AT NOON. Two somber, red-faced cops who looked ready to leave the moment they entered. The whole center came out to hear what they had to say. Even the little kids were quiet because they, like everybody else, wanted to know if it was safe to come to the center.

The cops began before everybody arrived and found a seat in the hastily-arranged folding chairs of the main hall. The policemen sat on the edge of the stage and didn't bother to introduce themselves.

One cop did all the talking, "Listen up, people. I think it's important for you to understand what the situation up here is."

Ron watched from the far corner of the room with his arms folded across his chest.

"There's a gang war going on and some of these guys have machine guns."

Finally, the other cop found the energy to speak.

"If we get a call from security here and we hear that somebody is shooting up the place with a machine gun don't expect us to arrive till it's all over."

"Yeah, that's right. You're on your own. We're not rushing here knowing the bad guys have automatics," the other cop said.

That was that. The cops got up to leave but Ron stopped them with a question.

"So what are we paying you for?"

"What?" one cop bothered to ask, checking his watch.

"We pay taxes like everybody else."

"We're being honest. That's the deal. We don't have the training or the manpower to deal with a gang war."

"Why'd you come? You're not here to help or protect us. You just want us to go away."

The cops didn't even glance at Ron as they left.

After that the center was just dead anyway. We couldn't pretend anymore that we were safe even from ourselves.

I wanted to work for the last check and have that much more money to start the school year but that was a dead issue after seeing Ron beat like a dog in front of his sisters and all the rest of us.

Crow was crazy and he was vicious, even more so than Walter or anybody I knew. I was signing my time card to go home for the day when I heard Ron's sisters shouting for help. I ran through the double doors to the parking lot and saw Ron on all fours crawling away from Crow who had a pool stick and was beating Ron so hard in the head that I thought it was going to burst like a cantaloupe.

"Stop him!" Tracy said to me. "He's going to kill him!"

But I stood there frozen, doing nothing while the buffed Crow, in skin-tight tank top, pounded Ron with the fat end of the stick. Penny found another supervisor who ran over and gingerly guided Crow away. Crow talked as though he was right for beating Ron.

"Wouldn't let me use his car. Talking all that shit like he's really somebody. He ain't shit. I broke his ass down."

Crow was breathing hard but he wasn't drunk or loaded, excited was all I could see. Crow held up the pool stick as if he wanted us all to witness what he did Ron in with. The sisters had sense enough to leave Crow alone and tend to Ron. I think if they hadn't, Crow would have clubbed them too.

We stood there in the parking lot waiting for help, as Ron floated in and out of consciousness. Campus security arrived with the paramedics. Crow was at the edge of the scene watching so none of us said a word about how Ron got thrashed. Tracy gave me a ride home, crying so hard she could barely find the road between having to drive and calming Penny who was crying harder than she was. Finally, Tracy pulled over in front of my house.

"Don't you go back there. Somebody is going to get killed."

"Yeah, you're right," I said, but it wouldn't be Crow, that worthless piece of shit. Crow would live; the rest of us, Ron or Tracy or some goofy kid or even me would be the ones to die.

Red Tide

GARVY WAS ON HIS PORCH READING COMICS. It was a hot, sunny afternoon and he was glad to be home from school. He hated junior high school, what a crazy place, too many gangs and guns and fights. School scared him so much that the doctor gave him little pills to keep him calm. He took a few of them, but he stayed nervous. The other day somebody had stomped Bobby B. to death for being in the wrong neighborhood. Garvy didn't know Bobby too well, but he had been at school a week ago and saw the guy shooting baskets in the gym. Garvy started worrying that somebody wanted to off him, but nobody wanted to off Garvy. He was just a rooti-poot that thugs would abuse but wouldn't bother to kill. Garvy knew he was getting a little too weird about the whole thing. Sometimes, when walking home from school, he wanted to shout "Brim" or "Swan" just to see if somebody was gonna instantly appear and do him in because he was crazy enough to shout another gang's name in Crip territory. Home and neighborhood were safety and he stayed right on his block because he wanted no trouble. Then Dennis Hat moved into the next block. Dennis was one of the leaders of the Crips, the one that didn't fight but would shoot, and Garvy walked the long way round to get his comics. The world was getting smaller and smaller and he had a feeling he was soon gonna be a house hermit, trapped indoors with books and the TV. Suddenly a loud squealing distracted him from his reading. A little banged-up Nova was flying down the street with the cops behind it, sirens blasting. He saw somebody stick his arm out the window of the Nova and fling a brown bag out of the car and continue to speed down the street, cop car still following. They both turned up the next street and were gone. Garvy watched the brown bag bounce against the curb and roll to a rest. Then Sidney appeared. Sidney was the fat man of the neighborhood. He wasn't a fighter or a ranker; he wasn't interested in open hostility. He had won position because of his ability to get along with anybody who was worth anything to get along with, and his ability to make anybody trust him completely. And once they did Sidney would get in on what was good, and leave the rest. Also, he had a great talent that made everything work. He talked better than anybody and knew everything.

GARVY WATCHED SIDNEY CAUTIOUSLY APPROACH the bag and snatch it up, and hurry down the street. First Garvy thought he'd just ignore the whole thing and keep on reading. The bag, the police would come back to look for the bag. He hurried into the house, not wanting to have to explain anything to the cops. At home, Sidney had the bag in his hand, and without even having to look into it, knew what was inside: drugs. What he wanted was some money so he could do what he wanted to do and that was to get high, to get a motorcycle and to get some dames. Now he could do all of that. He spread out on the bed the contents of the bottle, a couple of thousand bright red capsules were before him. Red Devils. And two bucks apiece for this action.

Sidney was in the dough. All the fellas wanted stums, take two or three and you were fucked up for hours. Soon, everybody who wanted to get high knew that Sidney was dealing and his pockets got big from all the buyers. He could afford to stop bumming from his mother, he got his chopper—a really beautiful bike, metallic blue, and on the gas tank was an airbrushed skyline of L.A. with flying saucers hovering above the city. Sidney got a new leather jacket and held court under the big pine tree, sitting on the fire hydrant, talking and making deals with fellas. Jude, Garvy's older brother, would hang out there, but he wasn't into dropping Red Devils. Willy and Rick, little Dell, and the rest of them would listen to Sidney, hoping he might feel generous enough to hand out a free Red Devil or two.

"Two for four, four for six, you can get a hit, what's it gonna be, boy?"

Things were going good for Sidney until one day he was sitting on the fire hydrant, talking to Henry, the neighborhood idiot. Henry wasn't all that dumb; he couldn't read but he could work wood and build motorbikes and he worked harder at shit-jobs than anybody else. Every now and then Henry would go crazy. Once he set fire to a house and watched it burn, waiting for the firemen to get there, and when they did he tried to help them put out the fire. They ignored him until one of them realized he might be a suspect, and humored him until the cops came and took him away. He did his time putting out brushfires at youth camp in the mountains.

Anyway, Henry was squatting next to Sidney, holding a beer Sidney had given him, listening to Sidney try and convince him to dig up his backyard for five dollars. Before Sidney found the pills, his mother had given him fifty dollars to replant the back-yard and lately she had been getting on him to hurry up and get around to it. Henry knew Sidney wasn't gonna pay him anything fair, but he needed money and didn't have anythhig better to do than tear up a whole backyard and plant new sod. What he liked was hearing Sidney go on and on about how much he was gonna make, and what he could buy with it, and for so little work.

"Yeah, Henry-Hank, you could get twenty-five beers, or fif-teen hamburgers, or see three movies, or you could buy three Red Devils. Man, that's a whole lot of cash."

"Cool, I'll do it. But you oughta give me one of those pills. I'm your partner. I deserve that."

Sidney gave Henry a sharp look.

"Henry-Hank! Are you trying to stick me? Man, after I tell you about all the things I'm trying to do for you. That's really rough."

All of a sudden Sidney's face went soft. He fell back and tumbled off the fire hydrant and landed on his ass and lay on the lawn, completely out of it.

"Sidney, you all right?"

Sidney didn't answer. He lay still, breathing regularly, eyes closed and mouth open. Henry bent down and shook him.

"Get up Sidney, the cops might drive by."

He wasn't moving. Henry tried lifting him but he was too heavy for that, so Henry left him there and went to look for help. He found it at Garvy's house.

Garvy was watering the lawn when Henry came running up. He was careful around Henry and wondered what that crazy look on his face meant.

"Garvy! Where's Jude?"

"Watching TV."

"Go get him. Sidney's knocked out on the lawn. We gotta bring him home."

Garvy handed Henry the hose and left him drinking thirstily from it. He found Jude lying in front of the TV watching the basketball game.

"Henry wants you."

"What he wants?" Jude asked without turning his head to look at Garvy.

"Sidney is passed out, on the corner."

Jude stood up and trailed his brother out of the house. Outside, Henry was shirtless and wet. He was hosing his head and grinning like the nut that he was.

"Sidney's up the street?"

"Uh huh, yep. He's knocked out," Henry said letting the hose fall, and, dripping wet, followed them down the street. Under the big pine tree next to the fire hydrant, Sidney was still unconscious. Jude grabbed one arm and Henry the other and dragged him to his mother's house. As they lugged him along Garvy could see that he had pissed all over himself. At Sidney's, they knocked and Mrs. Bluebox opened it. She saw her son being held up, piss all over his pants, slobbering.

"You boys been getting Sidney drunk all week. I'm sick and tired of you thugs taking advantage of him."

Mrs. Bluebox grabbed Sidney, lugged him through the door, flung him inside, and slammed the door behind her. Henry and Jude smiled. Garvy, who had waited on the sidewalk, asked what had happened.

"Nothing but drugs," Jude said.

Sidney wasn't much good for anything. Everyday he was fucked up, passed out on somebody's lawn or porch. Once on a holiday, Mrs. Michaels invited Sidney in for a bowl of gumbo. At a nicely set table, with Garvy, Jude, Jude's girlfriend, and Mr. Michaels there, Sidney sat down at the table and politely thanked Mrs. Michaels for the invitation, took one sip, and the pills he had taken earlier busted on him. He slumped down and his face plopped into the gumbo. Jude lifted him and his face out of the gumbo, and laid him down on the couch.

Soon the drug flow from Sidney stopped. He was too high from his own windfall to care about making any money. But some of Sidney's customers decided that if he wasn't going to make money, they could.

Mrs. Bluebox came home from work to her furniture all upside down and ripped apart. Nothing was stolen, as far as she knew. Sidney knew what was stolen and he was out on the street looking for it.

SIDNEY WALKED AROUND the neighborhood in such casual good humor that everybody took it for granted that he got ripped off for big bucks. Sidney was so polite and generous that he began buying beers for Henry-Hank, Jude, Dinky, even little Dell, the guy everybody figured had done the dirty trick to Sidney. Nobody said anything about the theft to Sidney, except it became a neighborhood joke to ask him if he had Red Devils for sale to see if he'd wince. He never did. He'd smile broadly and shake his head and open his arms as if to say "I wish I did," or "Red Devils, me?" A week or so later, the Red Devil talk was history, so Sidney decided to make his move. About 11:30 that night he walked over to Gumbo's and tapped on the window. In a few minutes Gumbo was out the back door buckling up his overalls.

"What's up, Sidney?"

Sidney sat on the wooden picnic table near the patio and offered Gumbo a cigarette. Gumbo reached for it, but Sidney darted his hand away.

"Does your daddy let you smoke now?"

Gumbo sneered and gave Sidney the finger and headed toward the house.

"Hey Gumbo, don't walk away mad. I've got a money-making deal I know you gonna be interested in."

Gumbo appeared back at the table.

"Money?"

"Yeah. You know I got a job pulled on me and I'm pretty sure it was little Dell. I want you to make sure."

"Me, how could I do that?"

"You know him. Here's ten dollars, try to buy some and find out where he keeps them."

Sidney stood to go. At the gate he turned back to Gumbo.

"Gumbo, I know you know how to pull a job. Bring back the information and it's fifty for you. Bring back the drugs and hey, straight up, we'll split the profits from what we deal. You'll be my business partner."

And with that, Sidney left. Gumbo sat in the backyard for a long time trying to figure out what kind of scam Sidney was up to. He wasn't the kind of guy to give anybody a fair shake. Sidney was probably out to set him up to take the fall on the job. Yep, he'd get the drugs and Sidney would threaten to dime on him to little Dell if he didn't take five bucks for his effort and shut up. Having thought it over, Gumbo decided to sleep on it and decide the next day.

The next day Gumbo found himself over at little Dell's, at a cardtable with little Dell and a few other guys. Gumbo could see that Dell was dealing and doing the same thing that Sidney had done—sampling the merchandise. Everybody at the table was too fucked up to play poker with any kind of sense, so Gumbo was making the big killing. He left forty dollars richer and with a good idea where Dell kept the drugs. He had caught a glimpse of Dell in the bedroom, bending down and looking under the bed. That night Gumbo went over to Garvy's. Garvy was in the kitchen watching TV and reading a comic while eating potato chips.

"Garvy, time to eat. Let's get a pizza. I'll pay."

"You'll pay? Sure, let's go."

Outside, they walked in the direction of the nearest pizza joint, but then Gumbo started to go out of the way, halfway through a dark alley and finally stopping at a fence.

"Dell got some money of mine. I'm gonna go get it from him."

"Why couldn't we have gone through the front? And I'm not going into Dell's. You know those guys don't like me."

"Just hang out here. I'll be right back with the cash and we'll be on our way."

Gumbo moved two loose boards from the fence and squeezed his way into the yard. Gumbo knew that Dell was at the poolhall and was likely to be gone for hours. Dell's mama worked at night so Gumbo knew the house was empty. He pulled his hooded beanie over his face and found an unlocked back window, and looking around the cluttered, weed-filled yard, found a milk crate and placed it next to the window and hopped into the house. Cautiously, he crept to Dell's bedroom. There, he took a penlight from his pocket and circled the room, searching through the chest of drawers and the closet. Finally Gumbo looked under the bed, and from there he pulled out a few rolled-up socks. The first sock had another sock inside. The second sock was the prize. Gumbo popped the rubber band around a three-inch roll of bills. He flipped through the fat stack as he hurried to the window and hopped out. After closing the window and tossing the milkcrate into the weeds, he returned to Garvy who was pissed off for being left in the alley for so long.

"Damn, Gumbo, I was about to split, you're just fucking with me, you're not going to buy me nothing to eat."

"Stop bitching, we're gonna eat."

Gumbo waved Garvy on so confidently that Garvy figured that he got the cash from Dell. He followed Gumbo a few blocks to a bus stop and soon enough a bus rolled up.

"Where we're going? You got bus money for me?"

"Uh-hum, we're gonna go downtown to get a real good pizza."

They got on and Gumbo dropped coins into the money well and Garvey followed him reluctantly to the last long seat on the bus. He knew it was the only seat for the be-cool types to sit on. But he wasn't cool, he was a square, unless he was hanging out with Gumbo, then he got the chance to mumble tough and thug-stare and scowl. Twenty minutes later they arrived downtown near a tiny pizza restaurant. Garvy noticed that the lady behind the counter wasn't happy about them walking in. She frowned at Gumbo.

"I owe you money right?" Gumbo asked with a big grin on his face. "I'll tell you what, I'll pay now so this time you'll know I won't be sticking you by coming up short."

He handed her a twenty.

"Yeah, now that ought to cover this super-size pizza and the three dollars I owe you on the other one. You can keep that five dollar change."

Gumbo swaggered to the table, Garvy trailed behind him, silently amazed at Gumbo's big tipping. The waitress brought the pizza and was still as unfriendly to them as she had been before Gumbo doled out the money, but that didn't disturb his good mood. Before the pizza had cooled he was pulling pieces off the pan and hot-potatoing them to his mouth, and chasing them down with big gulps of soda. He ate two pieces for every piece Garvy ate and gained speed as he went along. Soon enough the pizza was gone.

"Come on Garv, let's go. I wanna get some of them dirty

books from that magazine stand around the corner."

Garvy shrugged and they left the restaurant and walked through the empty downtown streets to the magazine stand. Under the suspicious eye of the white-haired owner, Gumbo picked up four particularly raunchy magazines.

"Go 'head and get something Garv, I'll treat."

He'll treat, Garvy said to himself. And with a rush of greed Garvy picked up a *Playboy* and then moved over to the science fiction paperbacks and got a handful of them and hurried to the comic books and picked up a couple of dollars worth. He knew he had probably gotten far too much stuff for Gumbo to pay for, but he figured it was better to get too much than too little. He walked over to Gumbo and found him flipping through *Pulsating Vibrations.*

"Okay, that's what you want. Here, take these two I got. I'll need something to read on the bus. You pay for them cause you look older than me."

Garvy took the magazines and Gumbo's twenty. The old man rang everything up, took the money, and gave the change back without a word. Back on the street, Garvy wondered where Gumbo was leading them.

"Garvy, you think we could get a girl? We could find one, you know, a real fine G and she'd take us both on and it wouldn't cost too much. Maybe forty for the two of us."

"A ho? I don't see any ho's. And we're too young, they're not gonna let us even if we paid them."

"If I see one on the way to the bus, I'm gonna ask," Gumbo said with conviction. Garvy hoped that they wouldn't run into any, but then again, he hoped that they would. And he started to wonder what kind of dough Gumbo had. Finally they arrived at the downtown Greyhound station. It was late and most of the bums were gone.

"What you here for? You going some place and leaving me stranded here?"

"Garv, you're my boy. I'll get you home."

"I'm not your boy! You got me out here, now give me some bus money to get home!"

Gumbo laughed at Garvy and stepped into the street and flagged down a taxi. He leaned into the driver's window and started haggling with him and after a short loud argument, he handed the driver a bill and walked back to Garvy.

"You don't have to catch no bus, I got you a serious ride."

"Why, what's up with you? You got so much money that you giving it away. Why you doing this?"

Gumbo grinned like a fat devil.

"Cuz you helped me Garv, we're partners in crime. I pulled a heist and you was the lookout man."

Gumbo pulled the wad of bills from his pocket and slipped two twenties from under the rubberband. Garvy dropped his books to take the money. After picking up his stuff and putting the money into his pocket, he glared at Gumbo.

"You robbed Dell's!"

"Yep."

"And you're leaving town."

"Uh-huh. I'm getting out of dodge. I'm going to visit Fresno, see my uncle. He always likes me to visit."

"Gumbo, I'm gonna get killed!"

"No you ain't. You're a rooti-poot. Nobody saw us. Just don't say nothing. Somebody might suspect me but so what, I'm gone."

Garvy shook his head and walked to the taxi and got in. It was the first time he rode in a taxi.

"See you Garv, stay cool and I'll see you when school starts."

Gumbo waved to Garvy as the taxi pulled away. Garvy watched Gumbo trot into the bus station. The taxi driver wheeled along the streets till they arrived on Second Street, far too soon for Garvy.

House-locked, house-bound, and worried. He came home just ahead of his mother who was getting off from working the late shift. Garvy took off his clothes and got into bed and began his long isolation. He was determined not to leave the house until school started, three months away. His mother and brother failed to notice his change of behavior for the first three weeks. And when his mother did notice, she made use of him by having him wash the windows once a week. His brother figured he wasn't very popular and had to stay around the house because he wasn't wanted anywhere else. That opinion started to color his dealings with Garvy. Garvy was reading when Jude came into his bedroom.

"Ain't you got any friends?"

"No."

Halfway irritated by Garvy's terse reply to his friendly concern, Jude wondered why he was bothering with his smart-ass brother.

"Go play some ball. You'll meet people."

"I like reading. I don't like ball."

"Man, you gonna go nuts hanging out here all the time."

"I don't care."

"You ain't never gonna see any girls."

"Girls?"

Jude walked out of the room disgusted with his little brother, and for the first time Garvy felt more confined than safely hidden away.

Outside, the neighborhood was wild with crazy happenings. Before Dell got his money stolen, he was making up the slack in the neighborhood drug trade by selling fast and cheap. It was a buyer's market and Henry-Hank was the first to fall from the plentifulness. Henry ran out of his foster parents' house, naked and wild off Red Devils. He grappled and grabbed at the air like he was a sumo wrestler and then he shot around the corner and saw a Sparkletts water truck parked on Third Street. All those glass bottles must have excited something in Henry because he started yanking them and flinging them down. The bottles made a great sploosh when they smashed on the asphalt. The truck driver came running out of a house, paper slips flying out of his pockets, to see what was happening. Henry, butt-naked, was busting the bottles and laughing, completely oblivious to the charging driver. The driver grabbed him and Henry, ornery from the pills, punched him so hard that he broke his hand hitting him. The driver was out so Henry squatted down and rolled around on top of the broken glass. Soon, a big crowd gathered to watch Henry from a respectful distance. By the time the cops came Henry was cut up and bloody, but surprisingly, he wasn't punctured too badly.

Dell's trouble was the other current event that had everybody talking. Dell always wanted to be a gangster, and he hung out with gangsters. He even thought of himself as a drug godfather, but when his payroll disappeared and he couldn't pay his dealers and his protection, they all suspected he was holding out on them. Dell was running for his life. People got used to seeing Dell breaking down the street with his ex-buddies right on his butt trying to catch him to kick his ass some more. Dell wore big dark shades and a low-brim hat to hide his black eyes and lumpy head. They probably would have killed him if he hadn't shot one of them before they got the idea to shoot him. He happily went to jail and luckily got transfered to a northern prison. If he hadn't been transfered, one of his ex-buddies would have tried to get somebody on the inside to kill him.

The neighborhood started to calm down. Sidney was even more the gentleman than he had been before. He bought a suit and took to getting up early in the morning and sitting on the fire hydrant under the big pine tree, looking very business-like and serious, to read the paper.

Garvy still wasn't ready to leave the house. He figured if Gumbo wasn't back in town there wasn't any reason for him to be outside on the streets. But Garvy did leave the house before Gumbo returned. Gumbo disappeared for two years.

Family Ties

MRS. MICHAELS AND GARVY ARRIVED at their cousin's house in the late evening. The sun was setting as they got out of the car and walked onto the steep hill. San Francisco sprawled in front of them. It was a pretty sight, rolling hills covered with lights, but it made Garvy feel lonely for Los Angeles. His mother unlocked the trunk and gathered their luggage. He watched, not wanting to help, wondering how long it would take her to notice that he was content to watch her work. He had been sullen during the eight-hour ride to the Bay Area. He was resentful of having been forced to accompany her on her vacation.

"Garvy! Get over here and help me with these bags."

He smiled at his mother's command. He was glad she noticed his mood. She pointed to the luggage that she wanted him to carry. He picked up the largest suitcase and walked quickly to the steep wooden stairs that led to their cousin's door. He set it down on the porch and turned to go back for more. The door opened behind him, but he ran down without turning to see which of his relatives it was. At the bottom of the stairs he looked toward the porch; it was Fred and Sam, the grandkids. The two boys watched, pointing and smiling, then ran down to help. Mrs. Michaels instructed them on what to carry, and into the house they all went.

Uncomfortable in the damp, musty house, Garvy closely followed his mother. His dour mood changed when he smelled pork chops frying. In the kitchen a short, coal-black woman was frying breaded chops in a large iron skillet, and a portly old man with a stub of a cigar in his mouth sat at the table reading a paper. Billy stood up and hugged Mrs. Michaels. Bessie turned around from the stove and gave her a hug too, and went back to cooking. Garvy stayed in the doorway and hoped nobody would notice him so he wouldn't have to hug anybody. Bessie pointed to him.

"That boy of your is getting big. I bet he wants to eat."

"Oh, yeah, he's hungry. Want to eat, Garvy?"

Garvy shrugged.

"I'm sure that boy needs to eat," Bessie said.

Before something could be decided, Garvy left the kitchen and went into the living room to watch TV with Fred and Sam. The two of them were sitting so close to the TV that they blocked the screen from his view. He didn't feel like asking them to move. He opened his tote bag and got out his comics and sat down on the couch to read. After a few minutes he was securely involved in the adventures of Daredevil. A while passed before he noticed the presence of someone standing in front of him. It was Fred. He didn't like Fred because Fred acted retarded and vicious, at least that's how he remembered him, and there he was standing almost on top of him.

"What you want?" Garvy asked irritably.

"What you reading?"

"A comic."

"Let me see it."

"I'm reading it!" Garvy said firmly and ignored Fred. He wasn't afraid of him, he was a lot larger than Fred, but he was still very leery around him. Suddenly his magazine was torn away from him. Garvy looked at the half a comic he had left in his hand. Fred was still in front of him but now he was smiling and quickly turning the ripped pages of the comic, looking at it with bug-eyed satisfaction. Garvy shot up and punched him in the nose so hard that he was thrown back over the coffee table and onto the floor. He got up slowly, looking surprised and hurt.

"That's what you get! Tearing somebody's stuff."

Fred rubbed his nose. The look of surprise disappeared and in its place was a wild grin. He sat up on his knee and grabbed a heavy glass ashtray and fastballed it at Garvy's head. Garvy ducked and the ashtray shattered against the wall behind him.

He jumped for Fred and Fred scurried away from him, heading for the door. Sam turned away from the TV and caught his brother by the neck as he tried to shoot past. Sam had him in a headlock and applied pressure until Fred was flat on his stomach and wheezing for breath. Sam slid on top of his back, and without breaking his grip, talked to him.

"Leave Garvy alone. You gonna get hurt messing around with him. Keep being a fool and I'll help him kick your ass."

The sound of a key unlocking the front door caused Sam to loosen his grip and let Fred go, but as he did, he said to him: "Don't say nothing to Mama or you'll get more of this." Sam hopped off Fred and as he did, he kicked Fred hard in the side. A whoosh of air came out of his lungs, and he lay gasping for air when his mother came into the room. Ann, the daughter of Bessie and Billy, looked in to see what was going on. She was dressed in an ankle-length leather coat and leather boots, and her hair was in a very large afro. She intimidated all three of them as she stood in the doorway. Garvy didn't know her too well, but she was always nice to him. After she hung up her coat, she saw Fred still lying on the floor. Then she noticed the shattered ashtray on the couch.

"Who broke this?" she asked.

"I don't know," Fred said with difficulty. He was still winded from the kick. Garvy and Sam were huddled next to the TV facing the set, but all their attention was directed to the scene behind them. Ann took Fred's chin into her hand, pulled his face close and sternly looked at him.

"What did I tell you about breaking Grandma's things?"

He shook his head slowly, trying not to anger his mother, but she dug her fingers deeper into his face. It was difficult for him to speak with his face tightly held, but he did.

"I don't know, Mama!"

"You do know!" she said and sharply slapped his face. He cried loudly and wildly. He thrashed about on the floor, putting his hands in front of his face to protect himself from more blows, but she was through with hitting him. She grabbed him by the arm and dragged him out of the room.

"She going to beat him?" Garvy asked Sam.

"Naw, she's taking him upstairs. Make him go to bed. He hates going to bed."

Garvy nodded and went back to reading. A short time later his mother came into the living room.

"Garvy, you have a pork chop waiting on you."

He followed her down the dark, cluttered hallway to the kitchen. Before they got there, she took his arm and pulled him close and whispered to him.

"Did you and Fred get into it?"

Garvy nodded.

"Watch the boy. He's a crazy so and so. Stay away from him, but if he tries something with you, bust him."

In the kitchen, Ann was at the table along with Bessie and Billy, but she wasn't eating; she was having a cigarette and coffee. Garvy sat down next to Ann and his mother brought over a plate for him and he started to eat. Mrs. Michaels gladly accepted the drink Billy had fixed for her, and she sat down to enjoy it. A little more relaxed, Mrs. Michaels decided to talk to Ann. She hadn't had a chance to talk to her yet.

"You're not too hungry, bet you're on a diet?"

Ann smiled and shook her head.

"I'm waiting on Sonny to call."

"Going out?"

"If he calls."

Billy interrupted their conversation by producing a deck of cards and dealing Mrs. Michaels into the game. Soon, Billy, Mrs. Michaels, and Bessie were looking at their hands. Garvy watched Ann smoke her cigarettes and occasionally sip her coffee. Something was wrong; Ann's mood soured as the game progressed. Garvy watched her slip into an evil state, glaring at her parents and hardly blinking to break the spell. He wondered how they could ignore her evil stare. She must be trying to start a fight, Garvy thought. Now, her eyes were slits and her mouth was set in a sneer. Ann grabbed the edge of the table and pulled herself close to her parents. Garvy had to lean away to not have his head under Ann's arm.

"Why won't you tell me if he called!"

Billy ignored her; Bessie flicked the ashes off her cigarette and gave Ann a stare that shut her up. Ann continued to lean forward, silenced but not willing to sit back. Bessie shoved her daughter into the chair.

"Don't crowd Lita's boy. He's trying to eat."

Ann sprang right back up. This time Garvy slid his chair aside.

"Why don't you people tell me anything? Did Sonny call?!"

This time Bessie ignored her and Billy gave her the cold stare. Mrs. Michaels kept her eyes on her cards. Ann sighed and sat back again in her chair.

"I'm tired of this mess. I'm gonna send the boys over to their daddy's and I'm gonna go with Sonny. Then you won't see me to fuck with me."

Bessie popped out of her seat and slapped Ann hard on the face. In trying to avoid the blow she leaned back too far and tumbled out of her chair. She got up screaming.

"You hate me! You hate me! I'm gonna go!"

Ann ran upstairs and a few moments later she was coming down with Fred dragging behind her, looking as sad as when she first dragged him up the stairs. She ran through the hallway calling for Sam. They heard him answer, and heard the front door open and slam shut, and the house was quiet. Bessie started talking in staccato mumbles about Ann. Garvy found it hard to understand her because she talked fast and bit off the ends of her words.

"Ann gets pills in her. Takes um and goes nilly-nuts. We don't know what to do with her. Then she goes and sees that Sonny, and you know he ain't good for nothing. I think he gives her pills. She wasn't so bad until he came around."

Mrs. Michaels stood up.

"I gotta put Garvy to bed."

Garvy was shocked; he didn't go to bed early in Los Angeles. Now he had to go to bed when something interesting was happening.

"Come on Garvy."

He followed her out of the room and caught up with her as she trudged slowly up the stairs. She was very overweight, and he could see that she was winded, but she wouldn't slow her pace up the steep stairs. At the top she paused and caught her breath, and then opened the door to the room where Garvy would be staying. She sat heavily on the bed and rested. It was a tiny room, with a single window that overlooked the multicolored lights of the city. Garvy sat down next to her.

"How come I can't stay up and watch TV? I stay up in L.A., how come I can't here?"

"Because this isn't your house and this isn't L.A."

Mrs. Michaels sighed; she had finally caught her breath.

"God, I hate these old thrown together cardboard houses with their steep-ass stairs."

She stood up to leave.

"You'll sleep and tomorrow I'll take you to the wharf and buy you a crab to eat."

After Mrs. Michaels was gone, Garvy was depressed, stuck in some place he didn't want to be. He took out his comics to cheer himself up. There, next to his bed was a clock radio; he turned it on and lay on the bed to read. One sad song after another came out of the radio, it was one of those stations that played only sad songs. It was raining. At first he wasn't sure, it was just a few drops striking the window. A song that he didn't know was playing. It was a really sad song.

It's a rainy night in Georgia,
Lord, I feel it's raining all over the world.
It's a rainy night in Georgia,
Lord, I feel it's raining all over the world.

Garvy was perfectly sad. He was even sadder and bluer than the man singing with his deep, mournful voice. He was so blue that he was happy to know that he could feel so sad. In the little room, with a sad song on the radio, he was good and sad, safe and secure in bed.

AFTER GARVY WAS OUT of the way upstairs, Mrs. Michaels came back to the table where Bessie and Billy were waiting. She picked up her cards and considered what she had been dealt. Bessie and Billy were tight lipped after the scene with Ann. Mrs. Michaels wondered what else was going to happen. Ann would be back sooner or later and when she did, something would have to happen. It was going to be a really big mess. She got good cards and won the next few hands. A winning streak started for her. Her winning seemed to bother penny-tight Billy. He puffed up a smoky cloud with the little stub of a cigar he had in his mouth. Bessie was concentrating too. Her face was mean in deliberation as she methodically shuffled her cards. Mrs. Michaels was getting a kick out of piling up the pennies she won in front of her. As the game got hotter, everyone loosened up and made conversation, and Billy was distracted enough to turn on the radio to his favorite big band station. When a Joe Williams song came on, Mrs. Michaels forgot about everything that was bothering her. She was collecting pennies in the card game, drinking Billy's expensive cognac and listening to Joe Williams' beautiful voice. It was late but they still played and Mrs. Michaels continued beating Bessie and Billy. Finally the fatigue of driving and card playing left her too drowsy to stay awake. From the kitchen they heard Ann come back into the house. She was shouting when she came into the room.

"He called! He called! But you people wouldn't tell me."

She stood in the doorway of the kitchen and was calm for a moment. She talked evenly at first, but her voice grew louder and louder, and her eyes were crazy with contempt.

"You don't respect me! You don't have any respect for me! That's why I hate you."

They ignored her and continued their card game. Ann watched them for awhile then left the kitchen.

"I guess her boyfriend is coming to get her?" Mrs. Michaels asked.

"Who knows about those two. She uses the pay phone at the gas station so nobody can hear their important plans," Bessie said.

"Important plans? Only important thing gonna happen between them two is her giving him her paycheck," Billy said.

Once again they heard the front door flung open so hard that it boomed against the wall and slammed shut again. Scowling, Bessie looked up from her cards toward Billy.

"What do you expect, the best thing to do is lock her out of the house."

They sat there and played cards without interest. Finally, Bessie dropped her cards and stood up.

"I'm gonna see if she's out there waiting on him."

Bessie turned away from the table and hurried out of the room. Mrs. Michaels looked to see if Billy, who was holding his cards in his hands ready to play them, had something to say.

"Why don't you make sure Bessie don't stay outside trying to get that stupid-ass girl to come in the house?"

She said sure, and went after Bessie and found her in the living room by the curtains. She carefully pulled the curtains aside and they could see Ann in her long black coat, smoking a cigarette, seated on the bottom step of the porch. As they watched, a big beat-up car stopped in front of the house. Ann sprinted to the car, opened the door and slid inside. The engine continued to run but the car stayed put. Silhouetted by the street lamp, Ann and Sonny twisted violently about in the front seat. Finally, the door on Ann's side shot open and she came falling out. She tried to grab the car door, but Sonny kicked her completely away from the car. She lay sprawled on her back and cursed Sonny.

"You can't get rid of me! You fucking son of a bitch!"

Ann charged back into the car. This time they heard a scream and Ann sprang out as if she was pulled by a rubber band. She came running and tumbling into the street, running for the stairs to the house. Bessie broke out of the daze she was in and yelled for her husband.

"Billy! Ann and Sonny are killing each other!"

Bessie pushed past Mrs. Michaels and ran for the front door. She opened the door and saw her daughter collapsed on the steps, crying uncontrollably. Mrs. Michaels stood at the front door and then ran down the stairs to Ann. She grabbed Ann by the arm and tried to pull her up. The car's engine stopped suddenly. Sonny got out of the car, slowly and stiffly, and walked unsurely to the stairs. Mrs. Michaels decided to go inside and find Billy. In the house, she looked in the kitchen for Billy, but he wasn't there. She knocked at his bedroom door; Billy answered it quickly, turned his back to her, and went over to the bed. He lifted the mattress with one hand, and with the other hand pulled out his gun from beneath it. He stuck the gun in the pocket of his baggy pants, and started walking for the door. She ran past him and blocked the doorway.

"Billy! Don't you go out there, you've got that gun and you're gonna end up shooting that boy."

"Lita, I'm tired of him always coming around. I'm gonna get him to go."

She didn't wait to see if Billy would listen to her; she ran ahead to see if she could get Sonny to leave. When she got out there, Sonny was at the foot of the steps, watching Bessie and Ann who were near the top.

"Look what your daughter done to me. She cut me!"

Sonny raised his hand. Blood streamed down from his hand onto his arm. He seemed to take satisfaction in his injury. Sonny rolled his jacket sleeve up so the blood could run free and not stain his clothes. Mrs. Michaels figured that Ann and her boyfriend were high on drugs. She never saw anything like this.

"That girl's out of her fucking mind!" Sonny shouted. Ann was still crying and was oblivious to Sonny. Bessie dragged her into the house ahead of Sonny, who was quickly moving toward them. He stopped and happily watched them hurry inside. Mrs. Michaels stayed on the outside because she knew that Billy was watching from the window, waiting and ready with his gun. She wanted to try and get rid of Sonny, but she thought it made better sense to call the police first. Maybe, if she left, Sonny would feel silly sitting out on the porch, yelling to himself. So, she went in. Through the door she heard Sonny yelling for them to come out. She was relieved to be inside the house. Bessie, Billy and Ann were on the couch; Billy was watching TV and puffing up an even bigger cloud than when they were playing cards. Bessie was holding Ann and wiping her face with a wet rag, then she led the now docile Ann upstairs to her room. Suddenly, Billy stood up and headed for the door. Mrs. Michaels finished her phone call to the police and saw Billy about to open the front door. She crossed the distance and squeezed in front of him.

"I said I'd get him to go."

She pushed him even further away from the door, and went outside to talk to Sonny again. Sonny, sitting down on the stairs, stood up and glared at her.

"Who are you? I don't know you! Where's Mr. Johnson? I want to show him what she done to me."

Mrs. Michaels was shocked to see that he was letting his hand bleed freely.

"You better leave. There's nothing around here for you. You just gonna get hurt."

"I'm not gonna get hurt, somebody else is gonna get hurt."

The blood running down his hand, dripping onto the steps, made her sick. She reached into her sweater pocket and took out her scarf and approached Sonny to wrap his hand. He jerked his hand away from her.

"I don't need no rag. I want to talk to the daddy. He's gonna pay to get me stitched up. I want some money or I'm gonna kick his ass too."

"Go away! He's in there and he don't want no shit from you."

"Lady, I don't know you. I don't know why you're out here talking to me. Go in the house and send out the daddy."

He pissed Mrs. Michaels off. He was standing near the edge of the stairs, swaying slowly to an inner motion. Mrs. Michaels was sick of the situation, and especially of Sonny. There she was, out in the cold San Francisco night, trying to keep Billy and Sonny from getting at each other. Fed up, she shoved all of her substantial weight against the precariously positioned Sonny. She sent him rolling down the stairs.

"Go! You half-headed fool!"

Sonny pulled himself to a sitting position.

"Stay there so I can get a pot of hot water to throw on you."

Mrs. Michaels went into the house and ran to the living room window and watched Sonny go slowly down the stairs. She looked for Billy but he wasn't around and neither were Bessie and Ann. Once again, she labored up the stairs to see if they were in Ann's room. She walked in and saw Ann lying on the bed on her stomach, her head buried in a pillow, crying softly. Bessie was next to her, rubbing her back. Mrs. Michaels gestured for Bessie to come to the door.

"I got rid of Sonny," Mrs. Michaels said. Bessie nodded and pulled at her sleeve.

"Lita, thanks for the help."

Bessie returned to the bed. All of them heard the shouting from the street; Bessie was at the window first. Ann and Mrs. Michaels fought for the space to see what was going on. Billy and Sonny were going at it. Sonny had something in his hand, it looked like a bumper jack. He was waving it at Billy and Billy was on the stairs, not backing away. Billy pointed his arm at Sonny and Sonny stepped back. There was a flash and then he fell.

Mrs. Michaels watched Bessie and Ann run out of the room and down the stairs. She went to Garvy's room and quietly opened the door and looked in. She heard the music, the radio was playing, and the bedside lamp was on. Garvy was sideways in bed, half covered, his head resting on a small pile of comics. Relieved, she turned the radio and lamp off and hurried out of the room. Downstairs, she was about to open the door and go outside when Billy burst through the door and ran past her to his bedroom. At first she thought to follow him but she decided to take a blanket off the living room sofa and see what she could do for Sonny. There, at the foot of the stairs, lay Sonny. Ann was kneeling next to him, her arms stretched before her, frantically rubbing his chest. His shirt was torn open, and his chest was rapidly rising and falling. Mrs. Michaels passed Bessie, who had her arms wrapped around herself, praying, saying the words of *Our Father*. Mrs. Michaels grabbed Ann by the shoulders and yanked her away from Sonny.

"He ain't dead! What you trying to do? Rub the bullets into his heart and kill him!"

Ann rolled herself into a tight little ball and was quiet. Mrs. Michaels took off her sweater, folded it and slipped it under his head. Even though it was night she could see the color leaving his face. Blood was draining from his wound into a widening pool beneath him. She wrapped the blanket around him, but it wouldn't do him much good; he was just about dead. Ann knew it too; she sprang up screaming and ran for the house.

"You people killed my boyfriend. I can't even have a boyfriend."

Bessie watched Ann disappear inside, then she dutifully plodded after her. Mrs. Michaels stayed by the body until the police came. Three cars arrived flashing blue, red and white lights that blinded her. Two officers cautiously approached; she heard them load and ready their shotguns. Their black uniforms backlighted by the lights, and their gleaming white helmets and shotguns had her scared and praying. She was so frightened that she couldn't bring herself to stand until they were before her and asked her to stand.

"What's going on here?"

"This man was threatening my cousin. Billy shot him."

"Where is Billy?" the other officer asked.

"In the house," Mrs. Michaels said.

"Will he come out and talk to us if you ask him?"

"He's just afraid, but he'll come out for me."

The policeman nodded, and Mrs. Michaels took off to the stairs. She turned to look at the scene before going into the house. One cop had covered Sonny with a white sheet and the other was writing in his handbook. Now, a small crowd of police gathered around their cars—shotguns out, looking around menacingly. She was determined to get Billy out of the house before they came in to get him. In the living room, Bessie had Ann under control. She was just about sitting on top of her, making sure she couldn't get away. Mrs. Michaels banged on Billy's bedroom door.

"The cops are here. Come out or they gonna come in."

Billy didn't answer. Mrs. Michaels patiently urged him to come out. When that didn't work she cursed and yelled until her voice gave out. She couldn't shout so she banged the door over and over. Still, he ignored her. Mrs. Michaels had given up on him coming out, then the door opened. There he was, standing calmly in the doorway, puffing his cigar.

"Billy, you okay?"

He nodded, puffing vigorously. Dressed now in a plaid jacket and a golf hat, he was ready to talk to the police. They passed the living room; Ann was asleep but Bessie was still on the edge of the sofa, guarding her. Mrs. Michaels waved to reassure Bessie. Billy, walking stiffly through the hallway, ignored Bessie and Ann. Outside, Mrs. Michaels nudged Billy to remind him to put his hands up as they walked down the stairs to talk to the police.

GARVY WAS IN A DEEP SLEEP. When the bed suddenly tipped to one side he woke up and saw his mother sitting on the bed looking at him. She was tired, her hair was mussed up and her clothes were wrinkled as if she had slept in them. She put her hand on his shoulder.

"Garvy, we're going. Get dressed, and come down to breakfast."

"Going? We're going? Why?"

"You said you wanted to see that haunted house."

"Winchester Manor."

"Whatever it's called. I'm gonna take you there, but first we're gonna get a motel."

Garvy sat up in bed and looked away from his mother toward the window to the blue morning and the rolling white clouds.

Mrs. Michaels pushed herself reluctantly from the bed.

"Hurry, I want to be in San Jose before noon."

Mrs. Michaels took his travel bag and left the room. Still confused from the early morning awakening, he sat on the side of the bed and waited until he was fully conscious before attempting to dress. Again, he looked out the window to the gorgeous blue day. Happy that they were leaving so soon, he dressed quickly, gathered his comics, and left the room. While walking down the stairs, he smelled bacon frying. Garvy was ready for breakfast and lots of bacon. He entered the kitchen; he saw Bessie cooking at the stove and Billy sitting at the table smoking a cigar. He had a bottle of liquor in front of him and a shot glass. His mother was seated next to Billy; she sipped her coffee and looked past Garvy, unaware that he was there.

"Breakfast ready, ma?"

Mrs. Michaels was surprised to see him standing in the doorway.

"Sure. Bessie just got to take the bacon off the fire."

Garvy noticed that Bessie and Billy hadn't said good morning to him. Bessie put the bacon on a plate and covered it with a napkin and placed it on the table. She smiled at him.

"Garvy, do me a favor, will ya? Go out and get the paper off the curb."

Garvy nodded and left the room. He left quickly because Bessie's cigarette, which always seemed to have lots of ashes on the end, wagged at him as she talked. It made him want to laugh but he knew that would get him into trouble. Outside, the chill of the morning air felt good. He walked down the stairs; on the brown wooden steps he saw tiny, dark red drops. He followed the drops until they lead to the sidewalk where there was a large stain that looked like blood. Somebody had recently hosed down the spot; the concrete was wet. It had to be blood. He got the newspaper and headed back into the house. Bessie, Billy and Mrs. Michaels crowded around the newspaper. Bessie's fingers nervously tried to untie the string around the paper. Finally, she grabbed her butterknife and cut the knot. She flipped through the paper and stopped at the news brief page.

"Here he is," Bessie said.

They huddled even closer and squinted.

"Lita, can you make this out?"

"Oh no. I left my glasses in the car."

"I can read it," Garvy said.

Bessie handed him the paper. He read it slowly, pronouncing every word clearly and loudly so that they could hear. He suspected that they could probably hear as well as they could see.

Sonny Clark of S.F. was shot and killed on 42nd St. 10:00 p.m. on Friday night. Witnesses say that he attacked a Mr. William Johnson in front of his residence with a bumper jack. Johnson shot Clark, who died at the scene. No charges were pressed.

Everyone sat back. Garvy finished his breakfast, wondering how he could have slept through a shooting. His mother stood up.

"Well, time to get on the road."

Bessie hugged Mrs. Michaels tightly. Garvy watched her cigarette bob and weave without dropping its ashes.

"Thanks, Lita."

Billy gave her a hug too, and they headed for the front door. Outside, as they walked down the stairs, he counted the drops of blood. He got up to thirty before they got to the bottom of the stairs. Everybody hugged once again, and Garvy and Mrs. Michaels got into the car and drove off. Garvy turned in his seat and watched Bessie and Billy waving to them as they drove away.

"Mama, something happened last night?"

Mrs. Michaels ignored him and fixed the rear view mirror.

"Somebody got shot?"

"Billy shot a robber. Now, shut up cause I don't want to talk about it."

He shut up. She would only get mad if he bugged her. That wasn't the truth, but he'd find out what happened, sooner or later.

Protector of Home, Hearth and Garage

WHEN GARVY AND HIS DAD walked into the garage to find a flashlight, Garvy noticed that the big engine jack was gone.

"Daddy, you think maybe Jude loaned it to somebody?"

Mr. Michaels took off his cap and rubbed his head with both hands. Then he started to make a barely audible *wheee* sound. Garvy could tell he was mad.

"Jude? Do you actually think that thick-headed, pot-smoking gump would loan something? Naw, one of his drug addict buddies done broke in again."

Mr. Michaels continued to maneuver around the junky, cluttered garage looking mad and mean. Garvy wondered how his father could find anything in all that junk, and for that matter how anybody would know where to look to steal. The garage was packed with transmissions, engines, bolts, fans, everything that had to do with cars, all sorts of tools, even license plates from around the country. Dirt was everywhere too, and what took up most of the space was two broken-down cars that Mr. Michaels had been working on for five years. Garvy didn't like the garage much, every time he went in there he'd stub his toes, get grease on his pants, or scratch his leg on a jagged car bumper. But his father knew what was there, and he was getting madder and madder as he took inventory of what was missing.

"Ah dog gawn! They got my tester, my power drill and my damn calibrator. Those little thick-headed thugs. I can't wait to shoot one of them. I'm gonna catch one of 'em coming over that fence, then bam!"

Garvy left the garage and walked to the house with the news of the break-in. This was the third time that the thieves got away with about a thousand dollars worth of stuff. At least that was what Mrs. Michaels said on the phone to her girlfriend.

She also said that Mr. Michaels was a dummy for storing his tools in the garage. Garvy liked all the excitement and hurried to inform his older brother Jude and his mother who were having breakfast. Garvy slipped through the door into the kitchen, pushing the two big dogs that followed him back into the yard. His brother and mother ignored him and he tried to look serious and mature when he really felt a lot of excitement.

"We got robbed again."

They both looked up,

"What?" his mama asked.

"They broke into the garage."

Jude left the table and walked into the backyard in his jockey-shorts and headed for the garage. A while later, Mr. Michaels and Jude came back in, looking grim.

"They got us again," Mr. Michaels said.

"I told you two not to put stuff back there, you don't need to have all those tools back there."

"But mama, how would daddy fix your car if he didn't have any tools?"

"Shut up, Garvy."

Garvy frowned and started re-reading the newspaper. Everybody was mad, and it was getting hot.

"Don't you have any sense, Jude? Why do you keep bringing those drug addict friends of yours back there so they can find out where we hide our things?"

"Daddy, they ain't my friends. There's a rock house up the street from us. And all those guys don't work, they hang out at the rock house getting high everyday. They need money so they go around the neighborhood stealing from everybody."

"Oh don't give me that bull, your best friend goes there to get high. I bet it's him."

"Daddy you don't know."

"I know all right!"

Mr. Michaels jumped up from the table and headed out of the door to the garage. Mrs. Michaels sighed, Jude looked glum.

"Sidney didn't steal those tools."

"Oh boy, shut up. You don't know who stole them, anybody could have stole them, you just don't know!"

Jude got up and left. Since he was alone with his mother, Garvy decided to make conversation.

"Mama, why don't they put up a bigger fence, or put up lots of lights back there, or bars on the windows?"

"Because they're stupid."

Mrs. Michaels pushed her chair back and got up from the table. Alone now, Garvy started reading the sports page. Mr. Michaels came back inside, looking even grimmer.

"They stole the hose, the water hose. Jesus Christ, they'd steal bullcrap if they could find it. Where's your mother?"

"I think she's getting dressed."

"Aw well. I wanted to tell her it had to be one of Jude's friends, probably that snot-sucker, Sidney, cause the dogs didn't bark."

"But the dogs always bark, and we don't go and see what they're barking at."

"Shut up, you just can't tell the kind of bark they bark when they're serious." Jude walked back into the kitchen. "It was your friends, the dogs didn't bark!"

"Dogs? Those dogs barked last night, I heard them bark, so what?"

"You heard them bark and you didn't look? You empty-headed gump!"

Jude threw his arms up and walked out again.

Mr. Michaels went into the yard again. This went on for the rest of the day, through the football games, dinner, TV shows and the late news. Finally, it was time for Garvy to go to bed. He undressed, got into his bed-clothes, and went to get a glass of water. His father was in the kitchen, sitting near the window, facing the yard, shotgun in his lap, hunting cap on his head.

"Daddy, I want a glass of water."

Mr. Michaels looked at his boy and grunted. He got up,

grabbed a glass, carried the shotgun to the refrigerator, poured out a glass of water and handed it to Garvy.

"Go to bed."

Just then Mrs. Michaels came into the kitchen in her robe.

"Winnie, will you put that gun up. Nobody's gonna come back tonight and shine a light on themselves so you can shoot them. Just wasting your time."

She turned and left.

"Daddy, don't shoot Jude, he might put his bike in the backyard tonight."

"Shut up. Go to bed. Jude's already put his bike up."

Garvy went to bed feeling safe, but before he dozed off, he heard his father snoring in the kitchen. For the rest of the night, he worried that somebody was going to climb over the fence and get him.

Love Land

EVERYBODY HAD A OPINION about Mama and Daddy's relationship. Some folks thought they were married but told a big lie, or that they got re-married but wanted people to believe they were broken up, or that Daddy still slept at the house but Mama was too proud to admit it. The root of these rumors is that Daddy wanted to give the impression that his dead-as-a-door-knob marriage was still in effect. Daddy was over every day like the mail unless Mama was on such a warpath that it would endanger his health to be on his former property. Then he'd do something that made me feel bad for him—like read his newspaper on the hood of his car in front of the house, or he'd disappear to visit his brother who lived on the other side of town, but he'd be back the next day like clockwork. The weekends were the most difficult for him because he couldn't cut out before she'd get home from work. Most of the time after breakfast I'd go out onto the porch expecting to see him parking the Galaxie 500. With paper in hand, Daddy would walk up and sit down next to me and without even looking he'd say: "How's your Mama?"

"Fine," I'd say.

"She's on the warpath?"

Like some meteorologist of my mother's moods, I made my daily report.

"Naw, she's okay."

"Oh," he said and went to the car and returned with a grocery bag. He rang the bell and I had to sit there as the buffer.

Daddy hoped me being there would make it possible for him to work his way inside.

"Hi, Lita. Here's some groceries."

I heard Mama hurumph and the screen door opened.

"Thanks," she said and the door slammed shut.

Daddy sat down next to me, slapped the paper once and unfurled it.

"Don't get that woman," he said and read the paper like he was going to read the ink off of it.

THEIR RELATIONSHIP HAD DISINTEGRATED into Daddy shouting and Mama hurling things at him. Once it was all of the knick-knacks on the mantle piece. I liked those knick-knacks, scenes from the Brothers Grimm stories; Little Red Riding Hood meeting the Wolf by a pond made of glass was my favorite. I admired the porcelain figures and fantasized at night when I slept that they unfroze and acted out the stories. But Mama flung them one after another at Daddy like cannon fire driving him to the front door and finally outside. It was pretty obvious he wasn't going to get his point across. More than anything Mama just didn't want to listen to him at all. Then it reached a point where I thought I might get hit with a stray knick-knack, or even something worse. There I was sitting at the table having a bowl of bean and bacon soup which I had to beg particularly hard to get because Mama thought the soup was overpriced and that she made better soup anyway. True, besides being salty it was tasteless. But I enjoyed the idea of having soup I selected for myself, until Daddy walked in and they immediately set in on an argument. Mama had started dinner and she was in the freezer pulling a big ham out. I don't know how Daddy saying, "You cooking that ham?" could make Mama so mad that she'd fling that big, frozen ham at him, but she did. The ham looked as though it might have enough lift to reach Daddy but it dropped like a rock, landing on, and shattering my bowl of soup.

"Come on, boy," Daddy said and grabbed my arm and led me out of the house. I was kind of in shock and didn't really want to go with him, but I didn't want to stay in the kitchen with Mama either.

Also, I knew what he was going to say. The same old tired

stuff about what Mama was up too. Then he surprised me.

"Your Mama wants a divorce."

"She does?" I asked. Hearing the word divorce made me feel feverish.

"Yeah. She wants to wreck the family. You want to see her do that?"

"No," I said.

"Then talk to her about it."

I nodded, but I knew I wasn't going to tell her anything. I didn't want them to divorce, but I wanted them to stop fighting even more.

We went to Norms and got burgers, but I didn't enjoy them because I knew Daddy was going to try to use me as a passport back into the house.

Later Mama gathered the three of us together to tell us that she wanted to leave Daddy. Winnie didn't seem to have much of a reaction. I was relieved to know that Daddy wasn't moving to New Orleans or something, just a few miles away. But Jude, he was pissed off. He didn't say anything as Daddy made a big production of gathering up his clothes and auto repair books. Jude just went and sat on the porch. Winnie followed and so did I. Mama stayed in the bedroom until Daddy finished putting his belongings into a duffle bag. At the front door he said, "Bye Lita," with such bitterness, she came out and stood on the porch in her robe and watched him start the car. Then he got out and started cleaning the windows like he did before driving anywhere.

"If any of you boys want to go with him, go ahead. I'm not stopping any of you."

Then I noticed Jude was crying. Mama saw it too.

"You, Jude. Go with him. I'm not stopping you."

Jude's head hung down. No one had turned on the porch light, so he looked like a dark ghost, crying softly to himself.

Daddy finally finished the windows and left. Mama went into the house. Jude and Winnie went up the street and I sat there wondering when I would see him again. Then I remembered it would be on the weekends, but I was surprised cause he showed up the next day like nothing had changed. Daddy drove up and waved me over to the Galaxie and handed me a couple of cabbages.

"Give these to your Mama," he said.

I nodded and brought them inside. Mama was on the couch watching television. She looked at the big greenish cabbages suspiciously.

"Where did you get those from?"

I don't know why she was asking. She knew already.

But it wasn't always Daddy confusing everybody. Mama's car would break and Daddy would appear to happily fix it. To all the world with Daddy hanging around all the time, having some but pretending to have all his meals at the house, it had to seem they were still together.

Still though, the pending divorce was hard on Daddy. His eyes were often red, and he looked worn and gaunt but that didn't worry me much. Mama knew what she wanted and got it—but Daddy, it was like somebody had pulled the rug out from underneath him. He was willing to do almost anything to stop the divorce, even if it meant having to ask a priest to come over and talk to her about excommunication. The priest appeared at the door one Saturday afternoon.

"Is your mother home?"

"Yeah," I said. "She's cooking."

"May I speak with her?"

"I dunno," I said and walked into the kitchen. Ever since that nun said I was retarded I didn't like any of those people from the church. The kitchen was steaming. Mama was boiling water, sweating in front of the sink, cutting up big hunks of cheese for fixing macaroni.

"Some priest wants to see you."

"A priest? Ask him what he wants."

I returned to the door but I guess the priest had gotten bored because he was standing on the edge of the porch, staring into the distance. I still didn't open the screen.

"She wants to know what you want."

The priest turned, startled.

"Oh, I want to talk to her..."

He must have realized I was ready to go back to watching cartoons.

"About the divorce, it's church policy to talk to both parties." Asking for it. That's what he was doing. Back into the kitchen.

"Mama, he wants to talk to you about the divorce."

"I told Winnie not to be sending any damn priests around to talk to me."

Mama dried her hands on a kitchen towel and tossed it onto the kitchen table. She walked to the front door and unlatched the screen door for him. The priest fixed a warm smile on his face. Least he wasn't dumb enough to confront her.

"Have a seat, Father."

"Thanks," he said and sat on the worn couch. Mama didn't sit next to him but instead on the recliner. She sat stiffly and upright as though this was a formal meeting.

"Lita, may I call you Lita?"

"Sure, Father."

"I'd like to talk to you about your marital problems. It really isn't too late to make your marriage work. That's why I'm here. Your husband has asked me, and I am a certified marriage counselor, to intercede to see if we can resolve the problems in your relationship."

Mama leaned a little forward in the recliner, still though, she was restraining herself.

"My ex-husband asked you to speak to me?"

"Yes, about the problems in your marriage."

"I'm not having problems in my marriage right now."

The priest smiled, reassuringly.

"Because I filed the papers. I'm going to be legally divorced. And I've never been happier."

"Happy?" the priest said as though he wasn't familiar with the word.

"I'm very happy. I don't think we have much to discuss."

"I think you should consider what you're doing to your family and to yourself. You are cutting yourself off from the possibility of reconciliation with your husband and with the church."

Mama sighed, stood up and walked to the door. The priest followed.

"If you don't reconcile with your husband, the church must sever its relationship with you. You will be excommunicated."

"Thank you, Father. That's fine with me."

Mama held the screen open for him.

"Really, Lita, I'm imploring you to reconsider."

"If I do, you'll be the first to know," Mama said and shut the door as soon as the priest was outside. Then she returned to the kitchen. After watching TV for a while, I went to the kitchen for a soda. Mama was sitting in one of the roller chairs, with her arms folded around herself, crying. Soon as she saw me, she stood up.

"What do you want?" she asked.

"A soda."

She turned quickly to the fridge, pulled a soda out and handed it to me. Unnerved, I quickly left the kitchen. It was one of the few times I saw my Mama cry.

Daddy took the divorce much harder. For a while it was all he would talk about. One day he showed up looking tense, like how he would after an argument with Mama.

"Hey, you," he said and sat down next to me. "I just came back from Mr. Lee."

"Yeah," I said. "He get another hunting dog?"

"Naw," he said.

Daddy sat there for a minute, and I realized he wanted to tell me something. His mouth opened a few times as though words were going to come out, but they didn't.

"I went over there and all the gun racks were empty."

Daddy stopped again and sat there, chewing air. Mr. Lee was a cabinet maker by trade and took great pride in rebuilding his modest little house into something really nice. His patio was made to resemble a cabin; log paneling lined the walls and his gun collection was kept in four walnut racks. Besides that, Mr. Lee had fixed up his backyard into a kennel, big enough to keep 12 hounds.

Daddy started talking again.

"So I went over there and Lee was sitting there watching the news. We watched TV for a while and I said, 'Hey, where're your guns?'"

He paused again and I had to nudge him on.

"Yeah," I said. "What did he do with them?"

"He told me he was having them cleaned, then his face got all serious. 'Winnie,' he said, 'I've been thinking 'bout how you and Lita busted up. You know if Mrs. Lee left me I'd be in sorry shape. That's why I took down the guns.'"

Daddy sighed and took off his hunting cap. "See, Lee, he's got his own mind 'bout things. He goes and pours himself a whiskey, (Daddy hardly drank at all, and didn't approve of Mr. Lee doing it.) and comes back looking sad as those hound dogs of his. 'Winnie,' he said, 'I had a friend, guy named Johnny. He was a crazy-tempered guy, but he was a good fella. Well, one day his gal just wanted to up and leave him and she did. Johnny got to be too grieving to want to be around, but his wife kept coming over to see Mrs. Lee. One day she came over and said to her, 'I saw Johnny when I was waiting at the bus stop to go to work this morning. He waved at me from his truck nice enough, like he was finally over being crazy about me leaving him.' Next day Mrs. Lee was all in tears, said that they found that poor lady shot dead at the bus stop. Johnny turned himself in and admitted he shot her. And you know he shot her with one of my guns. Borrowed it the day before. I don't believe he was in control of himself. He just saw her there at the bus stop and the next day took one of my rilfles and killed her.'"

Daddy put his hunting cap back on at such a crooked angle he looked like a doofus.

"What did that man think? I'm not some kind of crazy fool who goes around shooting his wife."

I knew not to say ex-wife.

"Then he tells me, 'I just don't want to see you make the same mistake.' Lee, I said, don't you worry about me. I'm doing fine. I'm not here to borrow a gun. Then he shakes his head like I'm lying and tells me, 'I believe you Winnie but I'm trying to keep the both of us from having any regrets.' I couldn't believe he'd say something like that to me."

I watched too many episodes of Alfred Hitchcock. Daddy didn't need to borrow shotguns. He had three of his own. Maybe he was trying to tell me something but Daddy didn't shoot Mama. I never saw him raise his hand to her. Mama, though, would occasionally hurl something at Daddy's head long after the divorce. Every now and then Mama would try to explain why she divorced him.

"Your father is the kind of man who makes you want to kill him. I didn't want to go to jail, so I got rid of him legally."

That seemed reasonable enough to me, and with Daddy being out of the house it was a relief not to have so many heavy things flying through the air. Over the months Mama gave more reasons for the divorce. One day she handed me the divorce papers.

"Here," she said and pointed to a line. It read: irreconcilable differences and mental cruelty.

"Your father was mentally cruel. That's reason enough to leave somebody."

I thought about that for a while. Daddy always said there was only one way to do something, the way he thought was right. That's why I didn't get the hang of tying shoelaces until I was in the fifth grade, or why basic math escaped me for years. Daddy tried to teach me those things. His method of teaching was okay if I had to trust him completely, and when there was only one way of doing something, such as swimming or bike riding. Complicated things brought out the worst in him. If he asked me for a 5/16 wrench and I couldn't find it, he'd yell, "It's the same as 10/32," and I'd be totally confused. Or sometimes I'd be reading and he'd sit next to me and scribble a math problem on a sheet of paper and shove it in front of my book. "Do it," he'd say. I'd smile and shove it back to him. "Don't know how," I'd say nonchalantly. He'd roll his eyes and snort.

"If there's one thing you have to know how to do in this life, it's long division."

I wanted to say maybe I won't know one thing in this life, but instead I pretended to scrutinize the math problem thinking that would be the faster way of getting rid of him. He made sure to guide me through each step of dividing six-figure numbers, even taking time to show me the old-fashioned way of doing it which entailed another set of steps.

Maybe that was the kind of thing Mama meant by mental cruelty.

But one night Daddy gave me some eggs to give to Mama so she'd feel obligated to invite him into the house for dinner, and Mama still wouldn't let him in. She said to me, maybe in defense of herself, "Remember how he would play the reveille to wake you up to go to school?"

"Yeah," I said.

"He'd do the same thing to me, even on Saturdays."

"Oh," I said, shaking my head. Maybe that's why Mama started throwing things at him.

That was the biggest difference between Mama and Daddy. Daddy never liked to draw attention to himself. Sure, he scowled a lot but his scowl looked more like indigestion than anger. He carried himself as though he was still a World War II Staff Sergeant, which was okay for a man with three big sons who towered over him. Daddy got his due of quiet respect, but Mama, she was the exact opposite. Her way of handling life's problems was to make so much trouble and noise that whoever or whatever was the problem had to back down. It was her personal creed, and she used it to great effect. Some grocery store clerk would slip up and overcharge her. Mama wouldn't politely bring it to the clerk's attention, instead she'd raise her voice, just to let him know who he was dealing with.

"Hey, you! This milk is only 89 cents!"

"Excuse me," the clerk said and took a look at the milk. "It's marked 99 cents."

Mama snatched it from him.

"It's on sale!" Mama's voice raised dramatically.

The clerk stepped back. The people behind Mama stepped back too. Startled, the clerk nervously reached for the store microphone.

"Price check on half gallon Springfield whole milk."

"Price check? I gave you the right price, you're wasting my time! Who the hell you think you are and you don't even know the price of your own milk! Call your manager cause I don't want to talk to you!"

He didn't appease her fast enough. Now, she was on a roll. I put down the *TV Guide* I was hiding behind, ducked under the grocery cart chain I had been leaning on, and slipped away. I didn't feel comfortably out of the line of fire until I left the store. From behind the big butcher paper produce advertisements I spied on the scene blossoming inside of the store. Mama was now shouting lustily at the manager as he helped the box boy load her bags.

She wheeled the grocery cart out of the store so fast that if someone got into her way that was their problem.

"There you are," she said and shoved the shopping cart to me. As I worked to guide the weighted cart up the inclined parking lot to the car, Mama smiled triumphantly.

"Those people had no idea who they were messing with."

I'm sure they didn't.

BECAUSE MAMA COULD PASS so easily, she got jobs and she quit jobs. If she felt a supervisor looked at her funny, she'd curse them out and quit right then and there. Daddy said she was looking to quit and it would catch up with her, but she said she could always find work. "Key punch operators are in great demand," she said smugly and Daddy had to shrug. His one retort was, "But what about retirement?" Mama would laugh and shake her head, "To hell with retiring."

Mama told me horror stories of how her co-workers would say vicious things about colored people. Once this stupid wig-wearing white woman said to her, "Those niggers just want to live off welfare," and how Mama didn't say anything. She just smiled and waited for the time when she could tell them all to go to hell. She quit cause she liked to quit and she could. And telling off racist white people who didn't know she was black gave her a special thrill. She told me about how on the last day of that job she cursed that wig-wearing white woman so bad she ran out of the office. Quitting was Mama's special power and she flaunted it over Daddy.

Daddy kept his job with the Post Office, though he was a certified mechanic, and loved numbers and could have had his own garage and done his own books. Mama complained bitterly of Daddy's lack of ambition. "Winnie, you act like the Post Office own you. You oughta quit and start a car repair business. Then you could stop working on people's cars for free." She told me a New Orleans story about how her brother the cop came across some boat motors and sold him one cheap. She said Daddy was ready to paint his boat and go out on the lake and then he heard her brother had gotten the boat motors from a fence. That did it, Mama said. He rowed to the middle of Lake Ponchatrain and tossed the motor over down to the bottom. "It was the kind of thing that made you want to toss him into the lake," she said, "always afraid of something, never taking a chance." Well, contrasted with Mama...

"Your Mama, she's always been angry. I just didn't know it

when I married her. Back then she was sweet and quiet. The way she talks now with all of that cursing and carrying on, she didn't do any of that. That's something she picked up out here."

Daddy came to believe that California somehow had corrupted Mama. That divorce and profanity had not crossed her mind until years later and sixteen hundred miles away from New Orleans. Mama was up front and proud of why she was the way she was.

"Somebody'd mess with me. Call me poor white trash and pull my hair. Steal my bread money. I'd go home crying and my Mama would whip my butt and send me back out there to get that money. You just got to knock people or they're going to knock you."

I figured maybe because Daddy was ten years older than Mama, he had the upper hand for a bit, but Mama had caught up and passed him. Everyone knew she was the one who ran the Michaels Family and that was fine with us. After a while even Daddy came to accept that obvious fact, acknowledging it with a gruff, "Better ask your mother," about everything more complicated than getting a hamburger. Daddy dropped hints for me to try to avoid his fate.

"You ought to date Mexican girls. They'll listen to you. They respect a man, but these women, women like your mother, you don't got a chance."

I was suspicious of his advice, as I was of most things he suggested. Then he said something that really made me nervous.

"See, I could have another wife. But I don't want another family. I can't see giving my name to some other kids. I just want you guys to have my name."

I had never thought about the family name before, specially when it came to worth. Maybe if there was some money attached to it, then maybe I'd be more excited.

"I don't think there's anything wrong with you marrying again."

Daddy grumbled, but he wouldn't get remarried.

After the divorce, Mama dated some rich guy who had a house up in the hills. He had a big party and Mama brought me along. His house was very fancy and he had a swimming pool and a tennis court. He was this short guy with a big belly who showed us the house like it was the first time he had seen it. I figured with all his money Mama had to marry him. But she didn't. He called but she wouldn't take his calls. She'd be on the couch with her legs up, eating potato chips, watching TV, usually her favorite position for talking on the phone, but she'd wave me off.

"She's busy," I'd say and he'd tell me to tell her to call but she never did. She told me why years later when I could no longer picture him.

"I didn't like how he treated you at his party."

"He didn't treat me any way. He didn't talk to me."

"Yeah, that's right. And that's why I stopped seeing him."

I guess Mama and Daddy were alike in that way, family first.

Getting the Goat

MR. VILLABINO STOPPED ON THE SIDE of the road to relieve himself. He and Gumbo were on the way back from Fresno. Gumbo thought the trip was taking too long because of his father's many roadside piss stops. It was early morning and frost was on the grass and weeds. Gumbo could watch the steam from his breath when he stuck his head out the truck window. His father liked his privacy and walked to a barbed-wire fence that wasn't too close to the road. Gumbo noticed that the fence was torn down further along. He saw something that looked like a goat outside of the fence. He hopped out of the cab to get a better view. He walked up to the animal and it stood its ground, chewed at the weeds and ignored him. Gumbo watched it for a while, then caught up with his father who was heading back to the truck.

"Pop, there's a goat over there," he pointed.

"That's not a goat, son. That's a sheep."

"Yeah?"

"You oughta know the difference, son. You gotta know your ass from up."

"I don't see goats and sheep, how should I know the difference?"

His father wasn't listening to him. He was looking around the back of his truck for something. He found a long piece of rope and a stick, and gestured for Gumbo to follow him. They walked over to the sheep.

"Hold the stick, if the sheep tries to get through the fence, hit it back this way."

Mr. Villabino made a wide circle to get on the far side of the sheep. With the sheep between him and Gumbo, he walked slowly up to it but the sheep took off for the gap in the fence.

Gumbo hit it hard on the back with his stick. The sheep lost its balance and tangled its legs in the wood and wires of the downed fence. Mr. Villabino tied the rope around the sheep's neck. The sheep put up a fight but Mr. Villabino managed to drag it along. Gumbo saw his father was getting red in the face so he whacked the sheep to hurry it up. Then he ran ahead and lowered the tailgate of the truck and helped his father lift the sheep into the truck. He quickly jumped out of the bed when the sheep was locked in. His father started the truck and was pulling it out on the road even as Gumbo was getting into the cab. Gumbo slammed the door shut.

"Why the hurry? People don't do time for finding sheep."

Mr. Villabino didn't say anything but he did shake his head at Gumbo's comment. Gumbo turned in his seat and watched the sheep out of the back window. When they got the sheep home they put it in the narrow space between the garage and fence. Mr. Villabino once had a pig in there but that was a long time ago. Afterward, they drove to the neighborhood markets and rummaged through the big trash bins for vegetables for the sheep to eat. Gumbo thought it was exciting, having a sheep in the yard, but he had been away for a week and wanted to go and find the fellas. He helped his father toss a big heap of rotten vegetables into the sheep's pen and went on his way.

After a few days Gumbo forgot about the sheep, but remembered the fourth was coming up soon. His father was getting ready for a big barbeque. The sheep was going to save them a lot of money. They had to get it ready a few days ahead of time because Mr. Villabino liked to soak his meat in wine for barbecuing. Gumbo was lying in bed when Mr. Villabino came into the room.

"Come on, son. Time to take care of that sheep."

Mr. Villabino watched his son get out of bed and put on his coveralls. He wanted to make sure Gumbo wasn't going back to sleep. After Gumbo was dressed they went out to the makeshift pen they had put the sheep in.

"All right, Gumbo, grab the sheep."

Gumbo straddled the sheep's back and held its head by the scruff of its neck. In Mr. Villabino's hand was a long knife. With quick sawing motions he cut into the sheep's neck. Gumbo expected anything but the sheep screaming like a baby. He didn't think a sheep could do that. His fathers hands were all bloody by the time the sheep stopped crying.

"Pops, I ain't gonna help you with the rest of what you got to do."

"You ain't! You telling or asking, boy?"

"Asking."

Gumbo waited, and watched Mr. Villabino get ready to tie the sheep upside down to drain. Then Gumbo searched around the yard until he found the ladder and climbed onto the flat roof of the garage. He had a plastic milk carton with peach brandy inside. He laid down on the roof and started drinking big, quick gulps of brandy. After he finished drinking most of it he decided to climb down. He got to the edge of the roof and looked down and changed his mind. He thought he might fall off the ladder. He saw his father washing up at the water faucet next to the back porch. He called to him.

"I'm not eating nothing that cries like a baby!"

His father shook his big head and laughed at his son.

"Boy, you'd eat a baby if it was cooked right."

Gumbo watched his father go into the house. Then he laid back and stretched out on the roof to take a nap. He knew he wasn't gonna eat any of that sheep.

Witches

HIS SISTER TOLD HIM IT WOULD BE a good experience. Madam Rose had those special powers of sight...she could tell him things about himself that he would never otherwise know. Gumbo thought this sounded like a lot of shit but his sister wanted him to go, and she was giving him the ten dollars. The problem was that she was taking him there for his consultation. His sister knew he would blow the money. She wanted to straighten his life out, so she gave him a ride to make sure he would get there.

Everybody had heard of Madam Rose. Once a month she sent groups of young boys to place 3 x 5 cards into the mailboxes of the people in the neighborhood. The cards had drawings of Madam Rose beside a crystal ball with ghostly figures rising up behind her, and information on how to contact her, and through her, deceased loved ones. Gumbo used to crumple those cards when he found them at the bottom of the mailbox. His sister, having given up on the church, found great comfort in Madam Rose's advice and counsel and made it a weekly event.

"Just drop me off on Western. I can walk the rest."

"No, Gumbo."

"You think I'm not gonna see her if I can help it?"

"Yes."

"Witches. What's she? A nasty old white lady, or something?"

"No."

"Good."

"I'm going to wait for you."

Gumbo sat quietly. He was stewing. He didn't say anything for the rest of the ride.

"Here we are."

Gumbo was surprised. It was a very neat little house that Madam Rose did her work from. You couldn't tell that there was a crazy woman doing business inside. But on the lawn she did have a big sign drawn up like those cards she had sent around.

"Go ring the bell. I'll wait in the car."

Gumbo did like she told him. He rang the bell and waited nervously for the Madam. The door opened and there in the doorway was a short, skinny, fair-skinned woman, dressed in black.

"Come in. I am of the spirit of Marie Laveau."

"Gina told me to come."

"Come in."

"Is it only ten dollars a visit?"

The old woman took him by the hand and led him inside the house. She told him to sit in a tiny seat that squeezed his thighs. The house smelled slightly musty, but not too bad. It was just grim, with photographs and paintings of people that were dead, he hoped. The people in the paintings were all wild-eyed, and the people in the photographs just looked sick. He wondered who they were, but didn't want to know. Madam Rose came into the room.

"I am ready to receive you."

She led him into a small study. The room had heavy curtains. It was very dark inside. There was a single candle in the center of the table. It barely lit up the room enough for Gumbo to find a chair.

"You cannot sit in that chair," she said from behind him.

"Shit," he said and hopped up. He sat down in the right chair and after a moment, smelled the incense. It was stronger than the incense at high mass. It was a sickly sweet smell and made him dizzy. Madam Rose reached over and took his hands and placed them on the table. She gazed at him with black, empty eyes. Her face was in flickering light, so her expressions changed from mad, to crazy, to mad. He thought she was going to do something nuts.

"Michael Vincent Xavier Villabino!" she shouted.

Gumbo jumped back and knocked the candle off the table. He gathered himself together. He heard her picking the candle up and lighting it and putting it back on the table. She grabbed his hands again.

"Michael Vincent Xavier Villabino!" she shouted again.

"What?!" he yelled back.

"You have sinned!"

Gumbo was shocked. This was worse than church.

"You went to jail recently."

"Yes."

"You committed a minor infraction."

"Stolen car."

"You have a heavy weight hanging over you."

"What?"

"It is in your future. It is foretold that you will be involved in a murder."

"Not me."

"You will be involved."

Gumbo wondered if she had connections with the cops.

"There is something that you can do."

"What?"

"It involves spirits, and devils. You are not clean, your soul is tarnished, it has to be cleansed, else it will be the devil's tool."

"What should I do?"

"Pray. But that is not enough. Next week I will begin the process of restoring your soul to its former glory."

"So if I pray you can help me out?"

"If you see me, I will work God's will."

Gumbo was relieved but still scared. Madam Rose led him to the door, collected her ten dollars, and made an appointment for him to see her in a week.

On the way home his sister asked a lot of questions. He just mumbled replies. He decided he would go to church that evening and do some praying. He wondered if he could just pray and not see Madam Rose. He didn't know if he could go back there. It was a lot easier going to church.

Pain

WALTER SPORTED A BLACK LEATHER JACKET like the Black Panthers and he treated women cruelly. The rumor was that he wasn't even good to his mother, Lady. The fellas used to say he talked back to her, demanding that she treat him like a man even before he was out of junior high. Mama said, "She ain't got a son, that boy gets treated like a spoiled husband. Ain't no good trying to buy his affection." Lady dressed him well and gave him a huge allowance but he was hardly home, choosing instead to drag the streets.

Walter was slick enough so that it seemed he wasn't dealing, even though at that time in black L.A. it was pretty hip to sell the occasional joint or even the frequent ounce and brag about being the dope man. Walter wasn't just slick. He was very smart. He had a genuine business sense, and most importantly, he understood and excelled at accounting. He got jobs at clubs keeping books so by the time he was twenty-one, it was rumored he was a partial owner of the "Complete Happening," the hottest nightclub on Crenshaw. Walter went from driving rinky-dink cars to very nice ones, Cougars to Chargers and eventually some years later, auto royalty, a Jag. Most people treated Walter with kid gloves except my big brother Jude, who didn't seem to care what Walter was or who he wanted to be.

I thought Walter's mother, Lady, was weird because she told us to never call her Mrs. or even Miss or she'd get angry. Even little kids called her Lady but they put a Miss in front of it. I heard she preferred to be called Lady because she was a beautician with a shop which had in bold letters across the front, "Lady's Shop of Beauty." Walter, even with all his talents, wanted that rep more than anything. He was unusual among my brother's friends. No one had a temper like Walter, no one was as sadistic, had as much to prove. That was the disease of my generation, where, seemingly, a good number of the kids I was growing up with decided respect was worth any price. Once when the fellas, my brothers and the half dozen or so of their closest friends, were over in the late evening, Walter came up in another new car, a Jag. A car more elegant than anything I have ever seen. He had a woman in the car with him.

"Hey, ya'll," he said, and pulled over. He got out of the Jag and went over to the porch but the woman stayed inside with the windows rolled up. I left for the comic store and was gone for a couple hours and when I came home it was dark. The fellas were in the house watching the Lakers. Walter was still there having a good time, yelling and laughing at the game with the rest of them. I didn't notice the girl. Maybe he took her home and returned. I went outside to see, and the girl was still in the car. First I thought she was a light-skinned black girl, but she wasn't. She was as white as somebody off the *Brady Bunch*. At first she tried to ignore me, but it must have become obvious that I was going to stand there under the street lamp and stare at her. She rolled down the window.

"Hi, I'm Miressa," she said.

"Hi, I'm Garvy." I wanted to talk to her and find out why she was sitting in a car for three hours while her boyfriend was in the house enjoying the ball game, but all I could do was stare.

"You're Jude's little brother?"

"Yeah," I said, but that was automatic. I was asked that at least once a day.

"You have nice brothers," she said smiling.

"Thanks," I said, then it occurred to me that she was probably thirsty.

"You want some water?"

"No, thank you," she said. She seemed kind of uncomfortable talking to me, as though it was wrong.

"I would…like to use your bathroom," she said suddenly.

"Sure," I said, and escorted her to my porch and opened the

door for her. At the door we heard arguing about the game, "Check out West! Bad-ass white boy!" and, "You don't know shit. He can't ball."

But as soon as I opened the door, silence. All of the fellas turned their attention to Miressa and then Walter. I didn't consider how Walter would feel about me bringing Miressa into the house. I learned fast, right there at the door. He flashed me a look of concentrated anger. The veins in his forehead popped out and his lips curled back to show his pointy incisors. And that was that. Walter went back to the game and Miressa smiled and waved at everyone. She bee-lined with a bowed head for the bathroom but she stopped and called to me.

"Garvy, the bathroom?"

I stood at the front door, paralyzed like I had been hit in the head by Walter's flash of anger.

"The hall. It's in the hall."

"Show her, Garv," Jude commanded and happily I did. I ran alongside her and led her nervously to the door and waited, feeling sort of like a dog. I heard water run and dribbling and finally the toilet flush. She opened the door but I forgot to move. Miressa looked nervous to see me standing there. She slid by me and headed to the living room where she hurriedly opened the door and returned outside. I felt bad, like I somehow made things worse for her. I followed her through the living room, making sure not to look in Walter's direction, but I knew he was looking at me as I slipped outside. She was back in the car, a shadow in the passenger seat. I walked right up to the car window and tapped. She tried to ignore me but I stood there until she unrolled it.

"What?" she said nervously.

"Huh," I said suddenly, without anything to say.

"You should go in," she said. Her suggestion got my mind back into gear.

"Why do you sit in the car?"

She frowned and turned away from me.

"You could sit in the back room, we got a couch in there."

She didn't say anything. She just continued looking away from me.

"You should go," she said.

I didn't want to make her mad at me but I wasn't going to leave. I lived there. My house was right across the street. I had a right to stand anywhere I wanted. Still though, I knew I was doing wrong, I was bugging her because she was this really pretty, exotic white girl straight out of the *Mod Squad*. How could I just leave and go around the corner to hang out at Gumbo's house? Then the front door of my house opened and I had a reason to go to Gumbo's. It was Walter standing in the doorway, looking at me. Then he started walking towards the car. I tried to nonchalantly walk away but he was on me in a second.

"Don't be hanging around my car," he said, and shoved me so hard I thought I was going to fall but I got my legs under me and kept going. I tried to avoid Walter after that, and I did for the most part. Walter continued to leave Miressa in the car, though sometimes he'd let her in and she'd sit in the farthest corner of the living room and keep her own company. She wouldn't even read or anything, or even look at anyone. It was like she was being punished for something. Things changed much later, when the fellas started settling down more or less. They started bringing their girlfriends by and Miressa had someone to talk to.

AFTER A WHILE IT WAS A TOPIC among us knuckleheads to conjecture on what Walter was really doing. He seemed to have a great deal of time to hang out with the fellas, that whole shooting hoops, getting something to eat, smoking joints, going on long drives, watching Sidney insult the dimwits and make deals thing, which seemed like a pretty exciting and satisfying way to spend time. We heard rumors about what he did when he wasn't around here. We knew he had a white girlfriend and expensive cars but no one saw his house except for Winnie, Jude and

Sidney, and they wouldn't say much. We heard little things: like it had white carpets, a big pool and it was in the hills. We also heard he had rental property, and for somebody just twenty-two, that was really amazing. He had a duplex around the corner. He didn't want too many people to know about it but we did. It was like anything else in our neighborhood—news seeped or exploded, but it got loose. Gumbo saw with his own eyes the kind of landlord he was. Gumbo said he was walking home from Santa Barbara Avenue and he saw Walter's car. Everybody knew his car cause he had "Walt" for a license plate. Gumbo said he hung around to see if he could bum a ride, even though Walter was more likely to kick him for leaning on the car. But anybody who knew Gumbo knew he would do anything to avoid walking four blocks. Anyway, he waited for a long time until he was about to start walking home cause it was getting late, when the door of one of Walter's duplex's flew open and Walter came storming out. Somebody was yelling at him from the house but Walter didn't say anything. He just waved them off. Gumbo stepped aside and had sense enough not to bother to ask him for a ride, probably cause he didn't want to get slapped. Walter unlocked the trunk and pulled from it a machine gun, an M-16. "Hold this," he said to Gumbo and handed the weapon to him as he searched through the trunk and came out with a big shoe box. Gumbo said it was filled with clips.

"Give me that!" Walter said, and snatched the gun from Gumbo and pushed a clip in. Walter went onto the porch and kicked the door, the whole time with the M-16 in his hands.

"Don't think I won't shoot! This is my house. I'll shoot if I feel like it."

Nothing. Gumbo said the house was quiet like you'd expect a house to be with somebody at the door with an M-16.

"Give me my rent. Don't make me come in there."

No response. Walter kicked the door once more and took out a key and tried it.

"Fucking deadlock!" he said, and stepped off of the porch,

firing off a clip into the sky. Then he went back and kicked the door for emphasis.

"I'm coming in!" he shouted.

Finally the door cracked open and an envelope slipped to the porch. Walter picked it up and walked out to the car. He put the gun in the trunk and started to count the money.

"He knows better than try to stiff me," Walter said, and slipped into the Cougar and drove away. It spread overnight, the M-16 in the trunk, threatening to shoot up his own place, threatening to shoot up a family cause he wanted his rent. His reputation was finally where he wanted it to be.

THEN WINNIE STARTED WORKING on Walter's cars, the fancy cars Walter kept turning up with, brand new but with something always wrong. Winnie was happy to work on them, as though rebuilding a head or a transmission could be fun. I don't think he even got paid for it. Walter wouldn't even help, sitting on a milk crate in a cluttered garage, afraid to move cause he might tear his leather pants or get some oil on them. It was obvious he was just using Winnie like most people did, but Winnie didn't see it. That bugged me more than any of the other things Walter did. Bugged me enough to get my butt kicked by him. One night Mama had it with Jude and Winnie. She knew they were letting the neighborhood eat off of us. She said before leaving to go to work, "Don't let anybody in the house. I told your brothers that if they do I'll throw them out for good!"

Mama always talked about throwing somebody out of the house and she was doing it more these days. I went to school and came home, changed clothes and spent the rest of the afternoon sitting on the porch reading comics. My neighbors, Kay Kay and Trice, were on their porches next door ignoring each other as they usually did. Kay was the oldest and treated her younger sister like she was brain damaged. I had a crush on both of them but they didn't pay much attention to me. I was thinking of trying to slip over there so I could watch them paint their nails and pop bubble gum. Before I got the nerve up to go, Walter's Cougar pulled up. He called from the car.

"Your brothers home?"

"No," I said, and tried to ignore him.

"I got to use your phone."

I shrugged, gathered my comics and bee-lined across the lawn to the sisters' porch. I hoped Walter would just drive off but he didn't. He cut his engine and got out of the car. He sported a new leather jacket with fringes under the arms and at the waist. He had a new hat, also black, one of those Clint Eastwood hats he wore in *Hang 'Em High*. Walter walked over to me with his hands in his pockets, trying not to make eye contact or even looking in my direction. Kay Kay and Trice both tried to act like it was no big deal, but they couldn't pull it off. They smiled nervously. I didn't think Kay Kay would get silly over Walter. She was four years older than me and Trice but she looked just as goofy as her younger sister.

"Garvy, let me in," he finally said, after starting down the street like anything would be more interesting than to talk to me.

"I can't."

"What do you mean you can't?"

"My mama said not to let anyone in."

"Oh," Walter said, and looked away again. I thought maybe I was off the hook.

"So, you gonna let me in?"

"Huh?"

Kay Kay and Trice were really enjoying watching me squirm.

"I got to use the phone. Come on," he reached over and grabbed my arm and yanked me up.

"No!" I jerked backward and pulled free.

Walter was surprised and backed off for a second.

"You gonna do me like that?" he said—something new, a different approach, being nice to me.

"It ain't me. My Mama said not to let anyone in the house."

"Yeah," he said, and pinned me with a cold stare. He stiffened for a second as though he was trying to calm himself. Then he turned to Kay Kay. "Can I use your phone?" he asked awkwardly as though he wasn't used to really asking for things.

"Yeah," she said and stood and pulled her short skirt a little higher. He didn't notice but I did. He followed when she unlocked the heavy wooden door and entered the dimly-lit house.

They didn't invite me in much and even though I had crushes on both of them, I didn't like going into their dark, cave-like house, but that was only part of it. Their father was most of it—a big man who didn't exude warmth. I'm sure if he was home Kay Kay wouldn't have invited Walter into the house to use the phone. Trice glanced up from painting her fingernails.

"Why'd you say he couldn't use the phone?"

"I dunno. My Mama asked me not to let anyone in the house."

She rolled her eyes and shifted around so she could look me square in the face.

"She's not at home. How'd she know?"

I shrugged, "She'd know."

The door opened. Kay Kay swept outside as though Walter was escorting her to the prom, but Walter ignored her as he had done before. He was cutting his eyes at me again with even more anger. As he walked off the porch heading for the car he turned to me and said clearly, "Fuck you and your family!"

I was big at thirteen, and I was finally starting to get some confidence, even a little temper. I should have let that confidence build for a while longer, but anger pure and hot boiled up and out of me.

"No, fuck you Walter!" I shouted and stood up. I wasn't afraid, not in the least. Not even when Walter turned and shouted at me.

"Don't say fuck you to me!"

The words rushed out of my mouth.

"Fuck you, Walter!"

He strode towards me, hands clinched into fists.

"I told you," he said.

"Fuck you!" I said, and stepped down the steps to meet him.

He hit me so hard I fell to one knee.

"I told you not to say it," he said, walking to his car. He drove away and I stayed there on the ground, sort of in shock.

"You're crying," Trice said.

"No, I'm not."

I tried to stand, but the ground seemed to be floating beneath me. Trice laughed at my dazed stumbling. I wanted to go home, wash my face in cool water and hide for the next week or so, but I stood there, dazed. Kay Kay came to me, I guess because Walter had finally driven away, satisfied that I wouldn't be saying any more "fuck you's." She took me by the hand and led me to my door and fished the keys out of my pocket and unlocked the door for me.

"That was dumb," she said and handed the keys back to me.

"Yeah," I said, finally capable of uttering something other than a series of "uh"s. I was glad to close the door.

I washed my red and swollen face and thought about how dumb I was. Now everybody in the neighborhood would know. I got my butt kicked in front of girls. I should have been embarrassed but I wasn't. So what if Kay Kay and Trice thought I was a pootbutt, some no-fighting wimp. It was Walter who was the chump, beating up on some kid. I remember the time Jude and Winnie were working on the Jag in the garage when Walter came rolling slowly through the alley in another of his fancy cars. This time he had a black girl in the car. She was light—light as Miressa, but she had that golden look, and her hair was oiled and pulled back into a tight pony tail. She and Walter got out of the car and they couldn't stop touching each other. Walter grinned stupidly and kept his hand on her waist. She looked like a *Soul Train* dancer wearing a midriff blouse and a miniskirt.

"We're going for a drive. Check the tires. I think one's low," Walter said to Winnie.

Walter and the girl turned to each other and started hugging and touching as Winnie happily rolled the compressor to the edge of the alley and snaked the hose around the transmission waiting to be rebuilt, the tool cabinets, the floor jacks. He checked each tire while Jude watched him, rocking contentedly on a milk crate.

"Let him check his own tires. This ain't a gas station," Jude said, but he wasn't serious.

"He'll have to buy me a beer," Winnie said, with that stupid grin. After all the tires were checked Winnie went back to working on the transmission. Walter and the girl were gone.

"Tell Walt the tires are okay," Winston said to me.

I wasn't going to tell Walter nothing. My brothers, yeah, they knew he jacked me up but they didn't think it was a big deal. Probably just me being a smart ass.

"Don't stand there, go on and tell him," Winnie said.

I shrugged and stayed put, but Jude shoved me.

"Alright," I said.

I left the garage and crossed the patio on the side gate. I hoped it was open so I could go out that way, through the front yard, but Daddy put on the padlock probably because Mama was on the warpath about Jude and Winnie's friends always cutting through our yard to the alley. The point was to make them walk the long way around to the corner. Now they just knocked at the door and walked through the house if Mama wasn't home. I pushed aside Toby, our big husky Mama got from her boss at work, so I could get the door open. I hoped Walter and his chick wouldn't be inside the kitchen. They weren't. Somebody had left the fridge open, so I tried to close it but a six pack was sticking out. Two beers were missing. Mama's beers. She liked Bud, while Jude and Winston hated it. Oh well, I thought. I'm not saying a thing, they can explain it. I headed to the front door but stopped when I heard something. A sharp noise like a yelp. I put my ear to the door leading to Mama's room.

"No, Walt!"

I felt it again, that rush of anger I felt before, the rush that got me beaten up. I wanted to open the door and see them on my mother's bed. I knew they were on the bed. Even if I was the youngest, I had to do something. I returned to the kitchen, and got a big knife out of the cabinet and sneaked through the hallway to Mama's room. The door was open and I could see the two of them on the bed and Mama's beers on the night stand. I could see his hunched back as he knelt above her. She was crying, whimpering as Walter laughed.

"Get off, please," she said. Walter still had his hat on, and his jacket, everything, but the girl, her skirt was around her waist. That's all I could see (because Walter was sitting on top of her). The knife I held in my hand seemed stupid somehow. I wasn't mad anymore, but excited, what I felt was new. I put my knife in my back pocket and went closer. Now I could see why she was crying. He was kneeling on her arms pinning them away from her body. The room was dark because of the thick curtains but light sneaked through, I could see her face, red and streaked from where he was slapping her not particularly hard, but like how Mama would when she wanted to sting me.

Walter shifted his weight and slid off of her, but it wasn't over, instead he slipped his hands around her neck as though he was going to choke her. I gasped when I saw her breasts, pale as she was. Walter turned and saw me, but he wasn't angry, he looked embarrassed.

"Oh, hey Garvy."

"Hi," I said.

The girl pulled down her blouse and straightened her miniskirt. Walter stood up quickly, clapped his hands and said, "Let's get out of here."

He yanked her off the bed. I waited in the dark room until I heard them in the kitchen going out to the yard to the garage. I hurried to the kitchen and peered through the window above the sink and saw them, the girl trailing behind Walter and

Walter ignoring her, walking angrily with his shoulders so rigid
and his legs so stiff, it looked like he could kill by looking at you.
I knew that girl wasn't gonna make it, not if she was gonna be
with him. Sooner or later Walter would do her up. The only
question was how bad was it gonna be.

What he did was put her in the hospital and she was never
the same, or so the fellas said. He raped and beat her, but what
happened to him was just as bad. Her brothers caught him and
beat him about the head with a claw hammer and put him in the
hospital for months. When he got out he was no longer the cool
tough guy. Last time I saw him he had all his stuff in a shopping
cart and he was gone. Whatever brain he had left must have
been pretty messed up. He reminded me of a clown with no
make up, just smiling and waving at people who wouldn't wave
back. Maybe they didn't know this guy in the raggedy clothes
and with the hair wild about his head was Walter. Somebody
gave him some money and he thanked them and kept going.
Gumbo said he saw him pushing that shopping cart onto the
freeway. Told Gumbo he was heading to San Diego to get a
fresh start.

Part Two: Local Color

The Arrangement

FRANK WOKE FROM HIS NAP BADLY. He smelled fish cooking in the kitchen. His aunt was making a lot of noise, rattling plates and pans and talking loudly to his brothers. Frank put his pillow over his head and tried to block out the racket. The noise came through. He gave up and decided it was time to go for a run. He got out of bed and quickly put on his sweat suit. Over to Cindy's was where he wanted to go. There he could get some rest. He walked into the kitchen and saw his aunt scurrying between the sink and the stove. He headed for the refrigerator, took out the orange juice, and drank it up. He watched his aunt in her bright red terrycloth robe move in tight, quick circles around the kitchen. She saw him looking.

"Frank, you drank all the orange juice?"

"No."

"You did!"

"All right, I did."

"Sit down and have dinner."

"I have to run."

"Over to that girl's house?"

Frank didn't say anything. His aunt was eyeing him. She had beady, little, penetrating eyes, and they always seemed beadier when she was out to get him.

"Somewhere, I'm going out to run. I don't know where I'm going to end up."

"Well, if I were you I wouldn't go over to that girl's house. I don't know if you're aware of this, but that girl could be a tramp."

"Could be," Frank said, and walked out of the kitchen. He was a little amazed at how his aunt didn't make him mad anymore. She could say anything now and it wouldn't get to him.

He opened the front door and breathed in the moist night air. He was glad it didn't smell of fish. He sat down on the porch steps to tie his shoelaces and stretch. It was a pretty Los Angeles night with a little chill in the air. He stood up and jogged off the porch steps.

He hated the start of a run; little pains and strange twitches bothered him for the first mile or so. But after that he could concentrate on his daydreaming. It was a long way to Cindy's. Frank liked the run if he could daydream the distance. He turned down Jefferson, a long and boring industrial street, and hurried along until he got to La Brea. He continued on his way, but a red light on busy La Brea made him hesitate. He slowed and judged his chance for crossing, then ran zig-zagging into the night traffic. He had to dodge one car and caused another to brake, but he made it to the other side and headed towards the foothills. At the beginning of the steep hill there were a few apartment buildings and a sidewalk, but these disappeared when the hill sharply angled higher. He had to run faster to keep his pace. That was the trouble with the La Brea hill—he never wanted to give up his pace. He wouldn't slow down unless it felt like his heart was about to pop. This time he had his rhythm, it would be easy going for a while.

It was turning out to be an alright run. He thought about how sometimes he was in pain running this hill, but now he was having no problem. Still, his body must be hurting, it did all those other times. He figured he didn't know he was in pain; it felt like he was having some kind of an athletic high. He wondered: did athletes drop dead from these highs? The idea of having a stroke on a lonely hill road made him consider the virtues of chess. He wasn't feeling euphoric anymore, not even good. He found himself laboring up the steepest part of the hill. All the pondering left him with a job of drudgery. Running became lifting one heavy foot and then the other. He did this until he had his second wind, and with the highest point of the hill close enough for a sprint, he muscled his way to the top. He passed the stop sign marking the downhill slope. He didn't slow any; he ran tilted back slightly, downhill faster than he thought was safe. The sweat he worked himself into felt good and cold as he ran with the wind blowing against him. The hill finally leveled out and he trotted as slowly as he could the short distance to Cindy's house.

Frank walked in circles around Cindy's front lawn. Every few circles he would turn to see if any lights had come on in her house—none did. He was having an extra-long warm-down. He didn't want to ring her doorbell. Nobody was home; the car wasn't in the driveway. It was too early for the house to be that dead. Finally he rang the doorbell, but as he thought, nobody was home. Cold and wet, he sat on a low porch pillar and decided to wait on her. This was fucked up, he thought. He had been coming over to Cindy's house in the evenings for a long-ass time. Now she raised up somewhere and he was stuck waiting on her. Frank was on the verge of leaving. He was going to wait for five cars to pass, and if none of them were the Jamesons', he was gone. After the eighth passed, Cindy's mama's car pulled into the driveway. Debra came out first, holding a dress. She walked over to him.

"See, Frank." She modeled it for him. "You oughta see the one my mama bought for Cindy! Boy, you look sweaty. Been running again?"

Frank smiled and said, "Yeah."

"Well, you oughta dry off before you get a chill," Debra said, and walked into the house. Mrs. Jameson and Brenda followed her. Frank gave Mrs. Jameson a perfunctory nod as she walked by. She ignored him. They were getting along as usual.

"Hi, Frank. How long have you been waiting? You ran?" Cindy asked as she shut the car door.

"Yeah, not long," he said coldly.

She pretended not to notice the tone of his voice. "My mother took us out shopping for school clothes. I was gonna call and tell you if you were coming over to come late, but I forgot.

My mother took us to dinner too."

"Yeah," he said as coldly as before.

"Come in the house. I got one of your t-shirts, you could take that wet one off."

Cindy took his arm and nudged him toward the house.

"I want to cool off. I'll be in after a while." He turned away and sat down on a step.

"You want me to stay out here with you? I'll put these packages up and be right back. Bring you a beer?"

"No, that's okay. I want to think about something. I'll be right in."

Cindy gave him a long, puzzled look and went into the house. She shut the door, and the image of Frank sitting huddled up on the porch stayed with her as she walked into the kitchen to check on the time. After that she went into Debra's bedroom. She saw Debra trying on her new dress. Cindy thought she looked too young in the bright yellow sundress.

"How do you like it?" Debra asked.

"Garvy would think you look fine," Cindy replied.

Debra paused and dropped her hands from the nervous work of adjusting the shoulder straps. She put her hands defiantly on her hips.

"What type of comment is that? If you don't like it, say so."

"I don't have an opinion about the dress, but I think Garvy would like it."

"I suppose Frank wouldn't like you in a yellow sundress? It would offend his taste in women's clothing?"

"I don't know about Frank, but I wouldn't want to go out with a girl who dresses like she's twelve."

Debra rolled her eyes and went back to admiring her dress. As Cindy was walking out of the room, Debra started talking as if to herself, but loud enough for Cindy to hear.

"You're some uppity cow. You come in here like you want to talk. I ask you about this dress (Debra lifted the front of the dress slightly and let it fall.), and you jump on me for no reason!"

Before Debra could get in more insults, Cindy left the room. She heard the door slam behind her. She went into the kitchen again, got a beer, checked the time, and headed for the front door. She opened it, expecting Frank to be gone, but he was still there. She sat down next to him. He stood up, she did too.

"Got you a beer," she said.

He took the beer, opened it, and had a drink.

"I'm not going to see you for a while, Cin."

"Why?"

"I'm just not."

Cindy sat next to him and watched him sip his beer.

"How long is a while?" she asked.

"Maybe a few days. I don't know."

"You want another beer?"

Frank sat silent and looked out toward the street. He could feel her looking at him, waiting for an answer.

"Yeah, if your mama doesn't mind."

Cindy quickly came back with a six-pack. She placed the pack next to him and pulled one off for herself.

"That's a lot of beer. Your mama is going to be bitching."

"I don't think so, there's another six-pack in there. It's such a nice night for sitting on the porch and drinking beer."

She noticed Frank hadn't picked up another beer, so she handed him one. After Frank finished that beer and a few of the others, he lay on the porch and tried to get himself together well enough to walk home. But Cindy moved close to him, and when she suggested they go into the house, that it was more comfortable than lying on the porch, he nodded, stood up, and looked towards the street as if he had somewhere to go.

Finally he said, "Yeah, let's go in the house. But I haven't forgotten what I said."

"I know you haven't," Cindy said.

Flight Control

"So when you think she'll be getting back?" Frank asked Garvy.

"Sometime tonight, it'll be too late for me to see her tonight, but first thing tomorrow."

"Well, I'm glad you're getting over all that broken-hearted crap."

"Yeah, I'm happy Frank, that you're happy for *me*." Garvy turned away from Frank and waved at Ronnie.

"Say Ron, why don't you hand me one of those beers."

Ronnie, lying comfortably on the thick grass of Garvy's front yard, wasn't going to hop up and hand Garvy a beer. It took a real effort for him to unclasp his hands that were pillowing his head and point towards the beer.

"Get it yourself big boy."

Garvy stood up, muttering about doggish partners and reached for a beer. He grabbed one and sat down again on the porch step.

"Why don't you go with her mama and meet Debra at the airport," Frank said to Garvy.

"You know how families are, her mama ain't gonna want me standing around when Debra and her are hugging."

Frank nodded his agreement. Garvy leaned back on the steps and rested his beer on his stomach.

"Have you seen Cindy today, is she going to pick Debra up too?" Garvy asked Frank.

"No, I haven't seen Cindy in a while."

"You two get in a fight?"

"No, I've just been playing too much chess to see her."

Frank stood up and bounced his basketball a couple of times. Then he practiced his jump shot until he got tired.

"You know, these last couple of days went by so slow. You know how it is when your lady raises up on you," Garvy said to nobody in particular.

Ronnie nodded to be polite but Frank sat down and looked at Garvy like he was observing a patient.

"Damn man, she's only been gone a week and a couple of days and you been bitching since day one. You must be in love for *days*."

"Yeah, I am. But you wouldn't understand none of that. You see, when you're away from the person that you're sharing your love with, it's just like missing an arm or something, and unless you're on the inside you wouldn't understand," Garvy said righteously.

"Garvy you're tripping, you're so in love it's hard to talk to you. If you're gonna be that in love, you oughta keep it to yourself."

Garvy sat quietly a while and then started talking again.

"Yeah, I bet sometime today her plane flys over my house."

"Well her plane won't be going over your house, she's coming from back east. She'd be coming from that direction." Frank pointed towards the mountains.

"You don't know, Frank."

"Maybe not."

Garvy looked down at Ronnie and noticed that he hadn't moved for a while. Sleeping away, he thought. It was warm and not too smoggy, a pretty good day for sleeping on the lawn. He didn't want to wake Ronnie but he wanted to talk, and it was almost too much work talking to Frank. He must be in an evil mood, Garvy thought. So Garvy sat there quietly sipping his beer and staring at the planes that occasionally flew overhead. After the fifth plane Garvy had to say something to somebody.

"Yeah, I'll be glad when that plane comes in."

"How do you know it's gonna come in?" Frank asked.

"It's supposed to! What type of question is that."

"Suppose something happened," Frank said.

"Ain't nothing gonna happen."

"Suppose it did," Frank said.

"You act like you want her plane to crash."

"I do."

Garvy was quiet for a long moment. He noticed that Ronnie was sitting up now, looking with interest.

"You mean you want her plane to crash."

"Yeah."

"You want her to die?"

"I didn't say that," Frank said.

Garvy was crying mad, he tried not to show it, but he was. He looked at Frank a long time and said, "If her plane crashes I'm gonna kill you."

Ronnie was watching with his head on his knees, he was wondering about his friends.

"What do you mean you're gonna kill *me*, I can't make her plane crash."

"But you want it to happen. If it does I'm gonna kill you."

Frank smiled at Garvy but Garvy didn't smile back. After a while Garvy went into his house and left them on the porch. They both knew he was upset, he never left them on the porch, he stayed outside till they left him or came into his house.

Ronnie stood up to stretch. Frank was about to ring the doorbell.

"Naw Frank, leave Garvy alone, you two do some weird shit. And that was some of the weirdest shit I've seen in a while. I'll call him up later and patch things up."

"I didn't mean to upset him like that, I didn't know he'd get that crazy. Shit, now he got me worrying about that plane crashing."

THE NEXT DAY DEBRA CAME BY Garvy's house, she brought him a cup with a whistle built into the handle, and some words on the front saying, "Whistle if you got to pee." Garvy thought it didn't make too much sense but he liked it anyway. And he never had a cup he could scare his brother with by whistling it loud and sharp at the breakfast table. Garvy and Debra sat on his front porch in the good summer heat, passing the time lazily —Garvy admiring Debra's skinny legs and Debra enjoying the attention that Garvy was paying her. After a while the heat got the better of them, so Garvy went into the house to get some lemonade. When he came out, Ronnie and Frank were on the porch. Debra was happy to see them and they were politely returning her affection. After they talked a while to Debra, Frank turned to Garvy.

"Hey, I have something for you," he pulled out of his back pocket a roll of comics and handed them to Garvy.

Garvy took them and sat down next to Debra.

"Thanks Frank," Garvy said.

Frank turned to Debra, "You know Deb, I'm happy you're back."

Debra called to Ronnie who was lying on the lawn again. "Ronnie, they've been at each other again?"

"Yeah. I don't think they can find nothing better to do."

Up and Running

GARVY AND FRANK WERE WALKING PAST the park, heading up to the sisters' house. The park was only two or so blocks long and only about a block-and-a-half wide; it formed a small valley, surrounded by four streets. They turned onto one of them and walked up till they saw Brenda. Brenda was the youngest of three sisters; Garvy and Frank had a running feud with her. There was something about her, a dumb look in her eye, but she was conniving enough to usually get her way.

Brenda kicked aside a ball she was playing with and ran up. She didn't look as if she could slow down and stop, but she did about a foot in front of them. "Hi," she said. She stood there blocking their way. "You want Debra and Cindy?"

"Yeah, we do. Are they home?" Garvy asked.

"Yeah, they're cleaning up. I'll tell them you're here."

She ran into the house. Garvy and Frank got to the porch and sat down on the steps. Garvy took up too much room so Frank sat down on the grass. A few minutes later Cindy came out the door. She had shorts and a halter top on. She looked hot from working in the house. "Hi," she said to both of them. She was happy to see them, the smile was stuck on her face. Frank stood up and took two big bounds and lifted her into the air, she kicked her legs and wiggled so he put her down. Garvy wanted to watch them play but knew it was time to go in the house.

"Cindy, is Deb in the house?"

"Yeah, she told me to tell you to come in. She's in the kitchen."

Garvy walked down the side of the house to the back door. He knocked lightly, the door opened.

"Garv!" Debra stood in the doorway grinning. Her voice was high and excited. "Come on in." She waved him inside the house.

"You want something to eat?"

"Naw, just ate."

"Not even a pickle? We have Claussens."

Garvy always had pickles when he came over, he knew she liked giving them to him. She walked over to the icebox and handed him the jar. He took one out and sat it on the table. She gave him a napkin to put it on. Garvy wasn't known for neatness.

A car pulled into the driveway, and a few minutes later Mrs. Jameson walked in.

"Hi Ma, what ya get?"

"Nothing much, just hot dogs for dinner."

"Mrs. Jameson, need some help with your groceries?"

"Hi Garvy, yeah, be careful with that big bag, there's eggs."

Garvy walked outside to get the groceries, and through the door he heard Mrs. Jameson ask what time he got there. His stomach started to hurt; he thought he would probably have to leave. Mrs. Jameson had bad weather moods. Debra came out the door. She ran over to him and hopped up on his shoulders.

"Mama wants to know if you and Frank want to stay for dinner."

Garvy smiled and said yeah. He liked it when she called her Mama—Mama and not my Mama.

"I'm gonna fold clothes so why don't you go to the park and throw frisbees with Frank and I'll come down in a bit."

"Alright. Hurry up and come on."

She went into the house and he started a slow trot to the park.

Garvy got to the park and looked around for Frank and Cindy. He walked over to the basketball courts and saw some tall brothers playing. Frank wasn't one of them. Garvy decided to run up the hillside to get a better view to find him. He headed toward the big elm trees and kicked at them, pretending he was Bruce Lee. He saw Frank and Cindy by the swings, sitting on the grass. He tried to sneak up behind them but Frank saw him.

"Aw, the weighty one is trying to sneak."

Garvy walked out from the bushes.

"Let's throw around the frisbee," he said.

Frank hopped up and was gone up the hillside. He was tall and long-legged, and so he bounded more when he ran. Garvy picked up the frisbee and threw it to him. The throw was long, Frank had to jump high to catch it. Garvy liked to make bad throws because Frank could still catch them. It was fun to watch. He couldn't jump like Frank but he could make nice diving catches. This was good to impress Debra with; he learned the secret of making the easy catch look hard. They threw for a while and then Debra showed up. Somebody threw her the frisbee. She ran after it and made a nice back-handed catch. She threw it back and called Cindy.

"We've got to cook since Garvy and Frank are eating over."

Cindy looked at Frank. "You're eating over?"

Frank didn't get along well with Mrs. Jameson. She knew he had strange late-night habits.

Frank asked Garvy, "You eating?"

"Yeah."

"Okay." Frank didn't like to make too many decisions. Garvy was always willing.

They headed back to the house. As they were walking through the driveway Garvy noticed that the girls' stepfather's car was there.

"Well Deb, Potbelly's home."

"Yeah, the first time this weekend, I was beginning to think he'd stay away till the divorce."

Garvy was scared of Potbelly because he drank a lot and wept all the time. He wept about how he was gonna lose his job, about his wife of two years leaving him because of his drinking and mostly because nobody in the house he owned would say anything to him except Brenda, and she didn't count. Cindy and Debra waited till he walked out of a room before they would go in. He never said much to Garvy, and Frank liked him, because he gave Frank a ride home and told him, "Women will kill you for nickels." Frank liked that sort of thing.

They all walked into the kitchen. Potbelly was sitting at the kitchen table reading the newspaper. He looked at them, waved and went back to reading. Garvy noticed he was sweating; he was drunk again. Garvy and Frank stood by the sink and the girls had a hard time getting around them to cook the hot dogs and fries. There was too much noise for Potbelly so he got up and went into another room. They all relaxed once he left. Then Mrs. Jameson came into the kitchen.

"How's everything going?"

"Okay Ma," Debra answered.

"I'm going to take a shower. Potbelly's getting some clothes. He'll be gone soon."

She left and Frank walked over to the table and had a seat. Garvy thought Frank looked sort of out of place—tall, hairy, and sweaty sitting at a nice dinette set. Cindy walked over to him and sat on his lap. Debra and Cindy had everything cooking so they had time to kill before dinner. Debra leaned against the sink with Garvy. Garvy put his arm around her and then twirled her so she was facing him.

Potbelly walked into the kitchen through the other door. He looked around, muttered something, and walked out. Garvy let go of Debra but Cindy didn't get off Frank's lap.

Garvy said to Debra in a low voice, "Did you hear what he said?"

"I heard something, couldn't make it out."

"You think he saw us playing?"

Debra didn't say anything.

Garvy held her hand, she pulled away, stirred the fries and gave her hand back. She turned her head suddenly towards the door. Garvy looked and saw Potbelly standing in the doorway. He looked mad and his face was damp with sweat. He stood there for a second and then walked away.

"Debra, I think maybe I should go."

Debra didn't say anything. She could see that Garvy was scared but she didn't want him to go. Frank and Cindy were laughing at some joke. They didn't see Potbelly the second time. Garvy watched Frank a while; he wondered if Frank knew what was going on. He wanted to leave but knew he wouldn't. He was still trying to let Frank know what was going on by staring at him when Potbelly came back for the third time. At first Garvy didn't know what he had in his hands. It was dark in the doorway but then he could make it out. He had a shotgun. He was looking straight at Garvy. At first Garvy didn't know what to think about the shotgun, then he felt his face starting to tingle like it would when he knew that he was gonna get hit. He wanted to cry.

"You gotta respect me and my daughters. I let you come over here and then you gonna put your hands all over them. Naw, it just ain't gonna happen."

He was talking in a low voice. Garvy stood paralyzed there next to Debra. He looked over at Frank. He couldn't look at Potbelly. Frank was standing now, Cindy was by his side. His eyes were as big as Garvy had ever seen them. Cindy looked at Frank and started laughing. Garvy thought she was gonna get them killed. Mrs. Jameson came back into the room. She didn't know what to do.

"Potbelly, put that gun down, you don't…" Her voice trailed off. Then Debra started to cry—and curse. For a moment Garvy wasn't scared, he was listening to Debra curse. He didn't think she'd be that good at it. She started in a walk but ended up running over to Potbelly.

"You stupid, you goddam stupid motha, you fool ass…"

She grabbed the gun from him and walked out of the kitchen into the street, threw it down and headed towards the park. Garvy watched from the porch and went back into the house. Mrs. Jameson was standing behind him. She pointed towards Debra.

"Go after her." Garvy said okay, and ran out the door. He

feld dumb having Mrs. Jameson telling him, he should of just run after her. Debra was running and walking and she was faster than he was so it took him a while to catch her. He put his arm around her; she swung it off. He tried it again; she did the same thing. She hurt him so he stopped trying. They were at the top of the park then. She was tired, so she leaned on the rail that went around the park. Garvy stood next to her. He noticed she had no sweater so he put his arm around her. She was still crying. For some reason Garvy thought she was mad at him.

"I took the gun cause I knew you wasn't gonna come over anymore. If you don't come it's alright. You know he's stupid, he wasn't gonna shoot anybody. I think Mama hid the bullets, trying to scare somebody."

She lost her breath; she was still mad. Garvy thought he should say something.

"You saved my life." He smiled half way, she gave him a blank look. Debra's Mama's car pulled up. Frank, Cindy and Brenda were in the car. Mrs. Jameson was smoking a cigarette hard. They got in; Garvy was sitting next to Cindy. She was smiling.

"Had you scared, huh Garv?"

"Yeah, what happened after we left?"

The inside of the car was dark except for the fire from Mrs. Jameson's cigarette. Garvy could hardly see Cindy's face. He felt Debra leaning towards him to hear what Cindy had to say. Garvy wished she would hurry up and say something because they were almost at his house.

"Potbelly went out to pick the gun up—Debra broke it though—he was pretty mad. Then my Mama started to scream at him; the fool grabbed his clothes and left."

"What Frank thought?" Garvy whispered.

"He still mad at me for laughing at him," Cindy said.

"Why were you laughing?"

"My Mama hid the shells to the shotgun in my drawer."

Garvy was quiet. He was thinking about how easy it was to

get shotgun shells. But he knew that if he had said that to Cindy, she'd say there was no gun stores in the neighborhood, or something like that.

DEBRA HAD HER PLATE BALANCED on her lap and was having trouble trying to balance the plate and watch the baseball game. The phone rang. She looked toward her Mama to answer it. Mrs. Jameson, busy with her own lunch, ignored the phone and her daughter. Debra put her plate on the floor and reached for the phone on the other side of the couch.

"Jean, let's talk. We oughta talk."

"This is Debra, not Mama. I'll get her."

She brought the phone to her Mama; she said quietly, "It's Potbelly. He's calling from your phone in the bedroom again."

Mrs. Jameson was chewing; she frowned, took a napkin, put it to her mouth and then balled it up and dropped it on her plate. She picked up the phone.

"I don't want to talk to you," she said and hung up. The phone rang again.

"Look, I'll let you get your clothes out of the bedroom. I'll let you come in."

Debra watched her Mama slam the phone down. Mrs. Jameson sat quiet and angry.

"Debra, we're going for a ride. Is Brenda still down the street?"

"I think so. You want me to get her?"

"Not yet—damn Potbelly, him and those phone calls."

Debra continued watching her baseball game; every now and then she'd look up at her Mama sitting tense and rigid. Debra thought about her plans to see Garvy and now they were replaced with duty, taking a long ride down the beach with family instead of lover. She brought her plate into the kitchen and walked past Cindy's room. She knocked and heard a muffled "What?" Debra opened the door.

"Wanna go for a ride? Potbelly's acting up."

"No, I want to sleep," Cindy said with her head under the sheets.

"Suit yourself." Debra went into the hall and saw her Mama with her sunglasses on and carrying her purse.

"You get Brenda yet?"

"You told me to wait."

"Get her. What about Cindy?"

"Sleeping."

"Leave her sleep. I can't do nothing with her anyway."

Debra went outside and saw Brenda playing tag up the street. She walked slowly with her message toward her little sister.

"Come on Brenda, we're going for a ride."

Brenda chased her girlfriend a final round of tag and followed Debra home. When Debra unlocked the front door Potbelly was blocking Mrs. Jameson's way out of the house. He was waving his arms and pacing between her and the door, shouting.

"Walk out—go 'head take your ass out!"

"I would Potbelly, if you'd get out of my way."

"Take your ass out!"

Mrs. Jameson paused and then headed for the door. She tried walking around him but he shoved her back.

"Okay Potbelly, stand there—you stand there till I get back!"

Mrs. Jameson ran out of the room into the kitchen. She came back with a carving knife, but Potbelly had disappeared into his car which was parked behind hers in the driveway. He tooted his horn as he pulled off and parked across the street.

"Mama, Potbelly's moving his car out for you," little Brenda said.

Mrs. Jameson and the girls got into the car and drove off. Potbelly waited till they turned the corner before getting out of his car and going into the house. He got a beer and seated himself at the kitchen table in his chair next to the window and tried reading the *Times*. He gave up and put his head on the table. After a while he sat up, finished his beer, and decided to go into his bedroom. He stopped at Cindy's door. He thought about knocking but didn't. He walked in and saw her twisted up in her sheets. He sat down beside her; she didn't move. She lay as if still asleep.

"What's wrong with your Mama? She can't talk to me. All she wants to do is turn you all against me."

Cindy continued laying still; he shook her.

"You're the only one who hasn't turned on me, why is your Mama doing this to me?"

Cindy rolled over and looked at him. "I don't know why she does anything. You married her."

Potbelly went on talking as if Cindy hadn't said anything.

"I don't want no divorce. I don't want to take this house from you. I love my family and she wants to take it from me. You tell me why, she's your Mama."

"You drink too much, you lost your job cause of it. She thinks you're gonna lose the house too."

Potbelly shut up and stared at Cindy. He was sweating from being drunk. Cindy smiled at him. Finally he leaned over and kissed her. She didn't move, she let him kiss her. She watched him and smelled the beer and gin he had been drinking. He pulled the sheets back; her short nightgown was high around her waist. She thought about pulling it down, but didn't. He put his hand on her stomach, she grabbed his hand, found his thumb and twisted till he took it off her. She turned her head and manuevered till she could sit up.

"Potbelly, give me a ride over Frank's."

Potbelly stood up, turned away from her and said yeah, as he walked out the room.

Potbelly could drive very well drunk. Cindy didn't say a word to him as he drove. He stopped at Frank's.

As Cindy was getting out she turned to him.

"Do you have any money, Potbelly?"

He looked through his wallet, took out a ten and gave it to her.

"Any more?"

He took out another ten, she took it, waved to him and walked to Frank's porch and rang the bell. She heard Potbelly drive off as Frank opened the door.

"Who was that?" Frank asked.

"Potbelly. He gave me a ride. Let's catch the bus to Foxhill. I can buy that chess book you want."

Frank said yeah, happy with the idea of getting the chess book.

"But I thought you were broke," he said.

"Potbelly gave me some."

"You gonna drive that man crazy."

"How can I do that? I'm the only one in the house that talks to him," she said smiling.

"I guess that's a shame," Frank said.

GARVY AND GUMBO STOOD in the dark of the alley. Garvy watched Gumbo reach in his heavy overcoat and pull out a silver .22. He gave it to Garvy. Garvy held the gun and wondered if it was loaded. He gave it back. Gumbo searched again in his pocket and pulled out a handful of bullets.

"I swiped them from my father," Gumbo said.

Garvy nodded and Gumbo loaded the gun. Then he stretched out his arm and aimed at a trash can. He fired and a loud crack sounded; it made Garvy want to go into his yard and say forget it. Gumbo gave a big round laugh.

"Don't trip Garv. By the time the pig gets around, we're gonna be in the house."

He laughed again and fired another shot into the trash can, then he bent his knees like they do on the police shows and emptied the gun, kicking wide holes into the can. He reloaded. Garvy watched him. Gumbo was fat. He wasn't real flabby, but was as solid as a tree trunk.

"Hey Garv, you gonna try this gun? We ain't got all night."

"Yeah, yeah, just give me the thing."

Garvy had never shot a gun before. He was leery of them. He aimed at the battered can and fired once.

"Yeah, Gumbo, this is all right. I'll buy it. Ten now, and I'll give you the fifteen next week."

"Why you want a gun, Garv?"

"I need one."

"What, school teachers out to get you?"

"Naw, it's Potbelly, he pulled that gun on me and Frank. I think he might go off on Debra and the rest of them."

Gumbo was silent. He handed Garvy more bullets.

"Man, you should stay out of stuff like that."

"What I'm gonna do, lay dead till Potbelly loons out on Debra? I might even be over there. This time Debra might not be able to get that shotgun away from him."

"I guess you gotta do what you gotta do, being a man and all that, but I wouldn't hang. Garv, you putting your ass on a firing range. I'll bet Frank is laying dead about going over there."

They walked into Garvy's yard. Garvy pushed aside his mutts and sat down on a weather-worn picnic table. Gumbo stood and stuck his hands deep into his pockets.

"You know Gumbo, it's Debra. If he goes off what I'm gonna do? Spit on him?"

"Naw, now you can shoot him. But if you murder his crazy ass, you ain't gonna be going to that college. They don't let murderers into college."

"What you think I oughta do?"

"Let her come stay with me," Gumbo said smiling.

Garvy stuck the gun into his drawer. He put the bullets in the pocket of an old coat and was relieved that he had the whole thing stored away. He walked into the kitchen to get a glass of water. His Mama called him from the backroom.

"Garvy, you want to go to the store and pick up some cake mix? I need some for work tomorrow. I have to bring a cake."

She was working on the sewing machine, hemming up a dress. He could bet that she was having a hard time with what she was doing.

"I'll go, want me to bring your purse?"

"No, take five dollars and the car keys."

"I can walk."

"I don't want you walking, drive."

"I'm gonna play some pinball at the bowling alley."

"Alright, don't use all my gas though."

Garvy got the money and headed out to the car.

Since he wasn't expected home in twenty minutes he could go over to Frank's. It was a cloudy night. He didn't have a jacket but didn't think he'd need one. He found a song on the radio and drove off. He was listening to Sly's "Somebody Is Watching You" when he suddenly felt like driving over to Debra's. But the fourteen miles over and back would have his Mama screaming his head off. Gas was something to be killed for at his house. He knew Debra was packing tonight; they were finally moving out of Potbelly's house and away from crazy ass Potbelly. The moving would take a couple days and Garvy was sure what would happen—Potbelly was gonna go off.

Garvy wasn't eating or sleeping. He was sick to his stomach. He knew that Potbelly wasn't going to let them move out of the house scot free. Garvy's imagination kept conjuring up a vision of Debra and her Mama carrying the last box out the door, and Potbelly hiding around a corner, axe in hand, waiting to get the last word in about them abandoning him. Garvy was getting hysterical. Debra told him don't worry, nothing was going to happen. She said if something did she could handle it. That was good enough for Garvy. He decided that until Debra moved out, he was going to be on the J.O.B. making sure Debra was safe. He called every three hours and went around there as often as he could bum bus money. He didn't see Potbelly much but when he did, Garvy was paralyzed. He didn't know why. It certainly wasn't Potbelly. Lately when he saw Potbelly he was drunk, sitting at the kitchen table in front of the window with the happy blue curtain. He just sat there reading the newspaper, looking small and shriveled. Garvy guessed he was scared of the guy because if Potbelly got excited he might suddenly get his health back long enough to run to his car and whip out his hunting rifle or something.

Garvy pulled in front of a rinky-dink house. Frank had been living with his aunt 14 years but had stopped doing work around the house in the last four. It was his twice-monthly duty to cut the front lawn and now with the lawn ankle high, Frank had a sense of success. His aunt would see he was serious about doing nothing. The little fat lady knew he wasn't going to lift a hand to cut the lawn or anything else but she thought, God willing, he might turn over a new leaf and do a bit of work.

Garvy went to the battered screen door and found it locked. He knocked, but not too hard. He didn't want the door to fall apart or come off its hinges. It didn't work; the screen door shook and rattled. He heard steps. Frank's aunt swung open the door. She stared at Garvy through the screen, then slammed the door shut. Garvy hated coming over to Frank's. Frank's aunt opened the door again a quarter of the way and peeped out hesitantly (glasses barely hanging on her nose). When she realized it was one of Frank's friends, she tried looking nice.

"Hi. Is Frank here?" Garvy said as politely as possible.

"Oh, let me see, one moment." The little fat lady wandered off, calling for Frank.

It was a couple of minutes before Frank showed up to the door. Even though it was getting colder, Frank had just gym shorts and a t-shirt on.

"Damn Frank, ain't you cold?"

"Me? Ha! I'm never cold. In the mind is where the cold comes from. I'm living a good clean life in touch with small animals and all sorts of rodents—make love to them, then eat the furry little things. Good for you, good to you."

"You wanna go to Jack in the Box?"

"Oh boy."

"But you're not tripping with me nowhere if you don't put some clothes on."

"Hey, what can I say. Be back in a second. Modesty prevails."

Garvy got back into the car. Frank was in top form tonight, which meant it would be almost impossible to get Frank to talk seriously about anything. So Garvy couldn't make them both depressed. Frank came outside with a bundle of sweats and a pair of worn-out tennis shoes. He threw them in the car and they drove off.

"When the last time you were around Cindy's?" Garvy asked.

"I was over there last night, and if you're willing to give me a ride, I'll go tonight."

"Just grease my palm with some money. I'm using all Ma's gas."

Going to the Jack in the Box was always like taking your life in your hands as far as Garvy was concerned, but it was the thing to do. Frank didn't care about the thing to do, he just liked to stay away from low-riders. But Garvy liked being scared. He turned into the parking lot, which was filled with Chevys and Pintos that had big Kragar mags. He manuevered his Mama's Dodge, making sure he didn't come too close to the parked cars. Then he stared at how packed the lot was. They went inside the brightly lit Jack in the Box. There was a long line to order food so Garvy stared at the people hanging around the inside. Most were loaded; some just looked kind of crazy.

The people that interested Garvy were the gangsters—the guys with the long coats and beanies or wide brims. Sometimes the gangsters toted canes and those gigantic radios they liked to carry. Garvy didn't really have a reason to fear most of them. Sometimes he worried about the crazy ones. They just did nothin'—not for profit or anything sensible—they just liked to screw up. Garvy didn't think he was stupid for hanging around places where these mad-dog types would show. He knew he could blend in. He could talk low, frown, and stroll like no tomorrow. The problem was if something did happen he didn't really know what he would do. He thought he might choke up. Frank didn't like to be bothered with any of them, but he liked the Jack in the Box fish burgers. Frank leaned over to say something to Garvy.

"Wow, we got a full house here."

"Yep."

"You know Garvy, I can't figure you. Why you like to come up to this crazy place when we could go to Fat Burgers?"

Garvy didn't say anything, it was his turn at the counter. He gave his order to a short, little, drill team captain from his high school. She knew who he was but didn't seem too interested in chatting with him. After Frank placed his order they went to sit down and wait for the food.

"You been helping with their moving?" Garvy asked.

"Not exactly, I'm doing more window hopping lately. I avoid Potbelly and Mrs. Jameson, too. It's late hours doing it this way but hell, it works."

"I've been going over there, helping them move. Tomorrow is the last day—a couple more boxes then the moving company comes for the big stuff," Garvy said.

"Hey Garv, nervous as your ass is, don't you feel funny about going over there as much as you're doing?"

"Not really."

"You're becoming a man among men. Maybe I'll go over there with you."

"Alright." The two of them finished their food. Garvy didn't say much because two girls with curlers and in robes were sitting across from him; one of the girls had her robe open to her upper thigh and Garvy was staring hang-doggedly. Finally Frank checked on what Garvy was staring at.

"Come on Garv, you're finished. Want to give me that ride now?"

"Yeah. Got some gas money?"

"I said I did. What do you think I am, bumming rides?!"

They walked out and drove off. Garvy started singing to a song on the radio till Frank joined in. Garvy turned the station.

"So you just don't see Potbelly?" Garvy asked.

"Yeah, if I can avoid him. No sense in taking chances."

"Do you think that he might go off again?"

"He could but I don't intend to be around."

"What about Cindy?"

"She won't be around either."

"You hope."

Garvy parked across the street from Cindy's. The house was next to a street lamp so it was well lit. Garvy started thinking about Debra, but he knew she was asleep.

"Thanks Garv, here's the two dollars I owe you."

"Anytime."

"Catch you tomorrow."

Frank walked toward the side of the house. He stopped at the first window, which was Cindy's, and tapped. The window opened and Frank hopped up and twisted his way inside. Garvy didn't drive off. He sat there and thought about Debra. He knew if he knocked on her window she'd be glad to see him. But Debra wouldn't want him to do something like that. She didn't like to take her Mama through changes. He knew Debra was different from Cindy, just like he was different from Frank. Those two never considered anybody but themselves. Garvy wondered if Debra liked him as much as her sister liked Frank. They didn't sleep together as much but Debra spent most of her time doing something with him, so he figured there must be some feeling there. Things were serious between him and Debra. But he wished he could tap on her window. It was getting late so he drove off to buy his Mama's stuff that he almost forgot about.

THE DOORBELL RANG. Debra put down the box she was trying to lift up to the table. She hoped it was Garvy at the door. It was accepted at her house that he did all the heavy lifting since Potbelly just sat around and stewed in his juices. She opened the door and was surprised to see Garvy with a trench coat on. She frowned at seeing him in the seedy, worn-out thing.

"Well, I'm happy to see you but your coat looks like you found it in an alley. You should've left it there."

"Gumbo gave it to me."

"Gumbo gave it to you. How's he doing?"

"He's alright. Just hanging out, acting fat."

Debra headed into the kitchen and pointed at the boxes stacked against the wall.

"Mama said since you're helping us out you can come with us to the seafood place I was telling you about."

"Okay. I'm gonna put this coat in your room."

Garvy walked into her room and closed the door. He leaned on the door to make sure nobody could get in and pulled out his .22. He opened the chamber to triple check and make sure it was empty; with bad little Brenda around he didn't want to take any chances. Then he wrapped the gun in some rags and stuffed it deep into one of the coat's inside pockets. He wanted to make sure it wasn't going to fall out. He glanced at Debra's nightstand and saw a thick paperback. He stuck that into the opposite pocket to act as a counterweight. He didn't want the coat slipping off the hanger. Then he hung the coat up in the closet. He tried to find Debra. He looked around and saw her talking to her Mama, who was raking the grass. Garvy watched them talking: skinny, tomboyish Debra and her Mama, who Debra took after in looks, except for her light brown skin. She walked into the house.

"There you are, spying on me and Moms out the back door window. Shame on you, Garv. Mama says if we hurry up, we can go and eat sooner and that Potbelly won't be around for a while."

"I'm not worried. I've been here before with him here and it's cool."

"Yeah, I know. It's just I know I wouldn't want to be around him if I didn't have to be."

Then she wrapped her arms around his waist. Garvy liked that but had to turn away so that the bullets in his front pocket wouldn't press against her. If she asked what was in his pocket he'd be in trouble. Lying to Debra about anything was sort of stupid, he couldn't stop smiling. Debra didn't notice, so they started loading boxes into the car outside. Garvy was struggling with a large, heavy box when Potbelly drove up. Debra was in the house getting another box, Garvy quickly stuck the one he was carrying into the car trunk and headed in. Debra was putting away a knick-knack.

"Your stepfather is home."

Debra looked up. She wasn't surprised, but she was concerned.

"We're just about through, Garv. He's probably just coming to get some more of his stuff for work."

"Oh."

"Garv, if you want to go to the park, I'll be down in a second."

"Naw, I'll help out. If Potbelly isn't drunk he'll be okay."

Potbelly walked through the door; he was drunk. Garvy suddenly figured out how smart Frank was about these things. Potbelly headed into the kitchen and sat down by the table with the blue curtain and flipped through some mail.

"Garvy, if you go it'll be alright."

"I'm gonna go get a box, be back."

Garvy walked into the kitchen past Potbelly into Debra's room. He got his coat off the hanger, leaned against the door, and pulled the gun out. Then he started to load it. He dropped a few bullets on the floor and bent over to pick them up. After he had the gun loaded he stuck it deep into his pants pocket and pulled his shirt out of his pants to hide it. He looked at himself in Debra's mirror. He could barely see the outline. He sat down on the bed and felt the gun poke him in the side. He ignored it. He thought about what he was doing. It wasn't that he was scared, even though he was, or that he had the gun. Garvy had a feeling, a hunch that Potbelly was going to do the do. Now, if the chump acted crazy Garvy could do something. But his stomach was telling him to head for the bathroom and throw up.

He had nothing to throw up, no breakfast. He was ready—you don't defend your love on a full stomach. The door opened; Debra came in.

"Hi Garv, I was looking for you."

She sat down next to him.

"Just thinking, Deb."

"Come on Garv, in a bit we're gonna be gone. You won't have to deal with this anymore."

"Yeah, but don't you think he might go off or something?"

"No, Potbelly ain't like that. He just talks, he's not gonna do anything."

"What about the shotgun thing, Deb?"

"I told you he wasn't gonna do anything. Potbelly doesn't do anything to anybody. Most of the time he just breaks down. He cries a lot but that's about it. He's a little man, Garv."

Debra stood up and left the room. Garvy didn't know whether to feel cheered up or not. Bunch of nuts, he thought. He helped Debra with a couple more boxes while keeping an eye on Potbelly. Potbelly sunk lower and lower in his chair until he was a sprawled-out mess. At the first chance, Garvy went into the bathroom and unloaded the gun. The drunk was dead to the world.

Doing It Up Right

"I DIDN'T GET THE CAR," Garvy said to Ronnie.

"Yeah, what're we gonna do?"

"The bus," Frank said smiling. He lifted Garvy's beanie off his head and fitted it on his own, like a Jewish skull cap.

"Yeah, the bus," Garvy said. "Fuck it, brother's eighteen, Moms won't even let him take the car. Muthafuck it! I'll call Debra."

Garvy grabbed his beanie off Frank's head and stuck it into his jacket.

"Naw Garv, don't call Deb. You two ain't got time for nobody else when you're together," Ron said.

"I don't care; I like to watch," Frank said.

They crossed the street and headed to the bus stop. The Arlington bus stop was nothing but a pole, so they stood around killing time. After ten minutes or so, the big R.T.D. rolled up kicking dust and paper wrappers into the air.

"This goes to Hollywood?" Ronnie asked the bus driver.

"Yeah, straight there."

"Thanks."

Frank and Ronnie sat in the seats near the rear that faced each other. Garvy made himself comfortable in the last long seat, and stared out the window and watched the red, green and yellow neon lights streak past the bus. He started to nod as he found himself lulled by the hum of the engine. Crenshaw was the center of L.A. as far as he was concerned, it was where the ladies hung out, it had the bookstores, the Chinese food places. The nice thing about Crenshaw was it wasn't where you were going, it was just where you had to walk, and since it was a good place to walk, it made the journey better. In the morning Garvy thought he'd walk over to Deb's. If he got there early enough he

could catch her when she still had her nightgown on. With that
romantic thought, Garvy nodded out.

When Garvy woke up, the bus was on Hollywood
Boulevard. He had a few blocks to go, so he sat quiet and
watched the Hollywood crowds. On a good Friday night everybody and his mama was out there. Chicanos, Brothers, silly
white boys, fags, ho's, and lots of pigs. Garvy, Frank and Ronnie
didn't come out there with any intentions. They were just interested in doing some passive observing. The bus came to their
stop on Vine. Ronnie looked back at old Garv to make sure he
was coming. Garvy sprang up trying to look alert and ready.
They got off the bus into a moving crowd. They ganged together and walked along till they could find a spot to stand and talk.

"What y'all wanna do?" Garvy asked. "Go on to Vito's or
check the movies?"

"Get something to eat," Frank said.

They headed in the direction of Vito's, Ronnie and Frank
talking as they walked, and Garvy trying to wake up while
checking out all the weird folk. Frank and Ronnie walked into a
record store. Garvy waited outside. He saw something he wanted to check out, a white girl waiting by the front of the store.
She had on a tight halter and a pair of ass-high shorts. Doo-da,
he thought, she wasn't that pale, and even though she wasn't
kept up, she had his eye. Garvy wasn't going to talk to her. He
was more than surprised when she walked over to him. He knew
she was going to ask him for some change or a dollar or something. He folded his arms and tried to look mean.

"Excuse me, do you know where I can catch the Crenshaw
bus?"

"Yeah, the bus stop's right down the street."

Garvy pointed.

"Thanks, I'm trying to find my sister."

"Where your sister lives?"

"Right off Crenshaw, around Rodes road."

"You know the neighborhood?" Garvy asked.

"No, I'm from up north, got in not too long ago with my boyfriend but he took off after we got here."

Garvy took his time in speaking.

"That's not a rough neighborhood but people over there don't see that many...hippie-looking girls around there."

"I'm not a hippie."

"I know, but people around there don't know that."

She paused and gave him a good long look. Garvy was about to do something, make a move or give her a line. But he wasn't used to that type of staring. He was getting embarrassed.

"Are you from around there?" she asked.

"Yeah, live right around there."

"How are you getting home?"

"Bus."

"Can I go with you, you know the area and I wouldn't have to wander around so much."

"Yeah, come on, I'll show you around that place, been living there for years, I oughta know."

Suddenly Garvy was nervous. He had this whitegirl going home with him or at least in the general direction. All he had to do was play it right and he'd have a little G-move on his hands. He wanted to do this up right. He had to get rid of Ronnie and Frank, and the easiest way to do that would be to leave them in the record store and explain the next time he saw them.

"You had anything to eat?" he asked her.

"No, not since a while ago."

"Let's go get a pizza or something."

"Okay," she said and they started walking. He slowed down a bit to get a look at her behind—kinda flat, he thought. Garvy looked up and they were in the middle of a crowd. Standing in front of them was the crazy black actor doing his routine. He had his portable record player on a small stand along with a few props; he was drawing big tonight. Dressed in a black smock and sandals he was entertaining the crowds by flapping and fluttering his lips to opera records. It was Barnum and Bailey fat men belting out a song, Garvy thought. When he realized he was with the girl he felt dumb checking out the guy with the lips. He put his arm around the girl to nudge her to leave. She snaked her arm around his big waist and Garvy wasn't thinking of the large-lipped fella anymore. They stood there a while and then moved on. Garvy felt awkward with her that close to him, he thought the world was looking. At least he knew he looked at Brothers who walked with whitegirls. The pizza place was up ahead and now Garvy didn't want to go in there, but he led the way in and searched for a table in the rear. After they were seated, a waiter got their order. Garvy sat there for a while and stared at the red checkered tablecloth. He was doing it up right. Show her you had a bit of money, be a gentleman and she was yours for two weeks.

"You know, I don't know your name," Garvy asked.

"Jean."

"Oh," Garvy said, waiting for her to ask his name but she didn't. "Garvy," he said smiling, pointing to himself.

"Garvy what?" she asked.

"Michaels."

She nodded and Garvy wished his telephone number was unlisted.

He stared when he noticed the waiter at his shoulder. He had a hot pizza he wanted to put on the table, then he brought the beer. Garvy and the girl started to eat. She ate fast and beat him to the last couple slices of pizza. He was upset since he paid for it and thought that men were always entitled to eat more anyway. With no food, he concentrated on the beer. He was trying to develop a taste for it.

"How come your boyfriend left you?"

"He didn't leave me."

He thought she was getting smart with him.

"What you doing here, eating with me?"

"I left him, he went to buy some hash or something, I didn't want to wait around."

"You gonna see him again?"

"I don't know."

"What does your boyfriend do?"

"He does a lot of hustling, and stuff like that."

"One of them dealer hippies?"

"No, he's not a hippie, he's like you."

"Like me, how's he like me?"

"He's black, but he's blacker than you, and he's taller but about your size."

"Where's he at now?"

"Probably looking for me."

Garvy was stone quiet. He didn't want to talk to her. On Hollywood if you minded your own business things were cool, if not, too many pimps and loons would mind it for you. Last time he was out there somebody got stabbed with an ice pick for messing with a pimp's ho. Suddenly Garvy was thinking about Ronnie and Frank, they were probably looking for him. Then an idea popped on him: Debra, wonderful Debra. He had wanted her to come to Hollywood with him in the first place. He'd call her up and maybe she could get the car and give him a ride. Then Garvy felt Jean's hand high up his thigh. She gave a squeeze and pulled close. Thoughts of Debra went bouncing down a hill somewhere.

"Thanks for the pizza," Jean said.

"Yeah, part of the job."

"You got a job?"

"Naw, go to school. Just a funny saying."

They left the warm pizza joint. He put his arm around her again, she did the same and stuck her hand into his back pocket.

"I got a joint," Garvy said.

"You want to smoke it?" she asked.

"If I could find somewhere we won't get popped, over on the side street. I know an alley way with some crates to sit on. Me and the fellas used to get high over there."

"Yeah, that sounds safe," she said.

Garvy knew what was happening; his dick was leading him into an alley. He didn't feel safe sitting in an alley with a bunch of dudes, let alone with one broad. But he didn't want to go home with her, whatever was going to happen he wanted it to happen here. They headed to the alley avoiding the crowds and Garvy watched for anybody that looked like her man. They walked into the narrow alley.

He found two crates and handed her one.

"Old drunks sometimes hang out in here, good thing it rained, don't smell so much."

"Yeah, where's the joint?" she asked.

Garvy felt insulted. He was going to say some more about the drunks, but she shut him up nice and neat. She didn't sit on the crate either, she leaned on the wall waiting for him to pass the fired up joint. He stood up to hand it to her, she hit it a couple of times and gave it back. Garvy was standing close; he put his arm around her and pulled her nearer. She pressed against him and they kissed. He pulled her halter up and went to work, she was kissing harder almost biting his lips. Now, he was leaning on the wall and she saddled his knee, he found the button on her shorts and tried to pull them down. She grabbed his arm and shook her head, then pushed him back and started rubbing him through his pants. Somehow she unzipped his pants and pulled him out hard. She rubbed a while longer then got on her knees. He stood there fooling with her hair; it was new to him, like her getting down on her knees and skulling him up. Finally he came and she spat it out and stood up wiping her mouth. He felt stupid, being in the alley and all. He didn't have much to say, so he fixed himself up. Then he started thinking about her man. She moved close to him and took his hand. She hung on to him and he thought she wanted him to say something.

"Your knees must hurt," Garvy said.

She looked down at her knees. "No, they don't hurt." She paused. Garvy couldn't see anything but her outline in the dark alley.

"You're gonna go home with me now?" she asked.

"Yeah, but I gotta find my friends, we're gonna meet up."

"My man is going to be trying to find me, you gonna come with me or what?"

"I'm gonna go with you but let me check for my friends. I'll be back."

Garvy kicked aside one of the crates and walked slowly out the alley. He could feel her looking at him walk away.

Garvy was jittery standing at the bus stop. He stared at the people passing by, checking for trouble. He was happy when the bus arrived. Then he thought maybe the girl was on the bus. Fuck it, he thought, it made more sense to get on than to hang around on Hollywood. He might meet up with her and her man, he could handle her but he didn't want no parts of a pimp. He got on looking at the seated passengers and bumping into people getting off. She wasn't on the bus. He sat down and tried to relax. Next outing he was going to deadass Westwood.

Clear Thinking

IT WAS RAINING. Garvy and Debra were on his bed, next to the window. They were naked and lying close. Garvy was counting to himself, he wasn't going to do anything more than what he had already done. He could get her clothes off, and get things started, but that was all. He lay counting, looking out the window watching the rain bead down the window pane. Debra put her head on his chest and wondered about him acting so moody and distant. Just because it didn't work right didn't mean she wanted to give up. Actually, she liked everything about fooling around, except for when he tried to hurt her. She knew he had to try, and she had to try too, but if he would stop, it would make things a lot easier for her.

"Are you mad at me?" she asked.

He counted to twenty, then said, "No."

"You shouldn't be mad at me."

"What should I be?"

Debra rubbed his chest, then kissed him. She slid her legs around one of his, and made Garvy pay attention to her. He was madder, then determined to be aloof, because he wanted his way and he wanted to get back at her. Because she started it, he wouldn't stop even for her yelping, even when he could feel her crying on his shoulder. Afterward she held onto him and wouldn't let him move.

"You okay?" he asked.

"It hurt," she said.

"I didn't mean to."

"Why didn't you stop?"

"I couldn't," Garvy said.

"Why? It couldn't have been fun, it hurt too much to be fun for anybody."

"You still hurt?" he asked.

"A little."

"You should take a bath. I read that hot water makes the hurt go away."

Garvy pulled away from her, found his pants, went into the bathroom and fixed her bathwater. He knelt down next to the tub and poured epsom salt into the water, and stirred the crystals around with his hand. He stood up and his mother's bath oil caught his eye. He poured some of that into the water, then sprayed some Lysol to freshen up the bathroom. He didn't want to go back to her. He told her the water was ready, stepped out of the now humid bathroom, but came back in to watch her get into the tub. She got in and sat there motionless, soaking. He thought she looked like an old lady. He felt strange, looking at her sitting in the tub and thinking about how unattractive she was. It was the way she sat in the tub. After football practice, his brother would come home and soak in a tub like she was doing. He got a washrag out of the hall cabinet, and decided he would wash her back. He knelt down behind her and started, as she sat there, not saying anything. He thought that next week he wouldn't see her. He didn't see how he could, she was nasty to him. He knelt watching her and thought if he was in love, he wouldn't feel that way. If you were in love, you wouldn't feel that disgusted with somebody. He decided he should be in love.

"How ya feeling, Deb?" he asked.

"Better."

He leaned over and started kissing her. She didn't return his kisses. But he didn't care, he was in love.

At The Movies

GUMBO OPENED THE FRONT DOOR and quickly ushered Garvy into the house. "Got a joint," Garvy said. He supposed Gumbo would be happy that he had something to smoke, but Gumbo didn't seem to care, he turned from him and walked into the kitchen. Garvy followed and saw him leaning over the sink looking out the kitchen window. Garvy wanted to see what was so interesting, but it was just the house next door, nothing unusual seemed to be going on.

"What are you looking for?"

"Nothing."

"You lonesome?"

"Naw."

"Just looking out the window?"

"Yep."

Garvy opened the refrigerator and took out the milk, he found a glass and poured himself some.

"You wanna smoke that joint?"

Garvy nodded and they went into Gumbo's room. Garvy sat next to the radio, turned it on and lit his joint, he took a hit and passed it to Gumbo, Gumbo took it and walked out of the room. Garvy picked a *Playboy* off the floor and looked through it, waiting for Gumbo to come back with his joint. After he finished looking at the pictures and cartoons he got up to find Gumbo. He was back at the sink looking out the window.

"Boy, you must be having some personal problems."

"Onla said he wanted to hit up my neighbor. He asked me to help."

"Yeah, what you said?"

"I told him no, I didn't want to go in on it, and I told him not to fuck around."

"What Onla said?"

"He told me to mind my business."

"Think he's gonna do it?"

"Uh-huh."

"He's got help?"

"Lil Stack."

"What you gonna do, Lil Stack is a Crip or something, ain't he?"

"Yep."

"So what you gonna do?"

Gumbo didn't say anything.

"I don't like fucking with them Crips, too many of them," Garvy said.

Gumbo continued looking out the window, he didn't look up at Garvy.

Garvy shook his head and left to listen to the radio. Gumbo pulled a chair up so he could sit and watch. After a while, Garvy came back into the room.

"I'm gonna split."

"Why you leaving?"

"I don't know. Tired of waiting around."

"Why don't you stay?"

"I don't know, I wanna go."

"You oughta stay."

"Why?"

Gumbo shrugged.

"Alright," Garvy said, and went back to the radio. A little later Gumbo thought he saw something. He got up and turned off the kitchen light. It was Onla dressed in black, sneaking along the side of his neighbor's house. Gumbo watched for a while till he saw Lil Stack, then called Garvy into the kitchen.

"Look at that."

"Look at what, why you got the lights out?"

"Lil Stack and Onla are going around to the backyard."

"They gonna break in?"

"Try to."

"What you gonna do?"

"Wait till they get inside and call the police."

"But Onla might know who called them."

"If he got sense he will."

After that Garvy was quiet, Gumbo knew he was scared, Garvy didn't want to be where he was, but Gumbo didn't mind, it was like having captive company.

"You wanna split?" Gumbo asked.

"Yeah, and get seen by one of those two, think I called the police."

"You're quick, run real fast they won't see you."

Garvy was mad, he wasn't saying anything.

"I got my weed under my bed in a shoe box top. Go roll a joint."

"I ain't your bitch, don't tell me what to do."

"I thought you wanted to smoke another joint, didn't say you was no bitch."

Garvy went to roll the joint. He came back and they smoked it in the kitchen.

"Onla is fucked up, expects to rob my neighbor. Shit, every-body gonna think I done it. Big time criminal Onla, break into somebody's house next door to him or around the corner. I hope they put the niggah's ass in jail, little punk."

Gumbo dialed the police on the kitchen phone. Less than a half hour later they saw two policemen run along the side of the house with shotguns.

"They got two more in the front yard, waiting for Onla and Lil Stack to break," Gumbo said.

"You think Onla got a gun?"

"I don't know, but I know Lil Stack keeps one."

Garvy stood away from the window thinking there might be some shooting.

"What the police are gonna do is wait for them to come out the house. Surprise them right in the yard when they don't expect it," Gumbo said, then got a beer out the refrigerator along with a package of salami. He handed the package to Garvy after he got himself a few pieces, and told him to get a beer if he wanted it.

"They should be coming out pretty soon."

Gumbo opened the window so that they could hear better. A short time later there were shouts in the yard, then what sounded like fighting. They could make out Onla's voice saying "Wait, wait, my hands are up." Then some more sounds like fighting, the police in the front yard came running toward the back to help, but there wasn't any need. They walked Onla around front handcuffed, it was easy to see that he was hurt, a policeman had to support him to keep him standing. Lil Stack didn't need any support, he was prone, two policemen carried him out of the backyard. Garvy and Gumbo left the kitchen and went to the front of the house.

"Don't go out yet, got to turn on the porch light like the old ladies do," Gumbo said.

Outside on the porch they watched the police put Onla in one car and lay Lil Stack in the back seat of the other. The police looked like they were in a hurry. They didn't want a crowd to gather.

"Let's go around to your house," Gumbo said.

Garvy nodded. "You think I should tell Mrs. Cobb they took Onla away?"

"How would you know, me and you been at the movies."

Something New

RONNIE PULLED HIS HONDA 150 alongside the curb, lit a cigarette and looked. Well-kept streets and freshly-cut lawns were as
far as he cared to see. He sat on the curb under the shade of an
elm till he finished his smoke. Then he walked to a door and
rang the bell. After a while he got tired of standing and was
deciding between ringing the bell again or sitting down on the
steps. Then Cindy opened the door.

"Oh, Ronnie." She stepped back to let Ronnie into the
house. He tried not to pay too much attention to her. She had
on a white terrycloth robe that was wrapped tightly around her.
Then he thought forget it, and grinned.

"Took you long enough to answer that door."

Cindy rolled her eyes. "You oughta be glad I got the door. I
was in the shower. A woman can't even get clean around here."
She smiled. "Frank's in my room. You can go in if you want." He
watched her head off to the shower, then he walked away. He
knocked lightly on the bedroom door and opened it. Frank was
sitting up in bed with his hands spread out on the blanket. His
fingernails were freshly painted brown, he held his hands up to
show Ronnie.

"How you like them?"

Ronnie stared, smiled and stuck his hands into his pockets.

"They're fine. Since when you start painting your nails?"

"Today. Cindy was painting her nails, so she ended up
painting mine."

"Yeah," Ronnie said, pulling up a beanbag out the corner.
He rolled around till he was sitting comfortably.

"You see Garv' today?" Frank asked.

"Yeah."

"He's acting crazy. I'll be playing with him and he goes *off,*
having a fit."

"Garv's alright," Ronnie said flipping through a bunch of Cindy's magazines.

"Yeah, Garv's alright. But sometimes he *trips*."

"He'll calm down." Ronnie shrugged. He wanted to change the subject. "Are you gonna stay here all day?"

Suddenly Frank's voice boomed out over the little room.

"All day, all day, here?!" He looked around the room trying to look disgusted. "Why should I stay here? Just because the little woman loves to fool around? Or that she feeds the fella well? A man, a real man, has to do what he has to do! Soon as my nails dry I'm gonna split. Cindy's sisters are gonna be here soon."

"You wanna go to the library?"

"Yeah, let's get some food. Won a couple of chess games. I'll pay some of what I owe you."

"Okay, but we go to the library first. Pizza slows the head down like a brick."

Frank nodded, tossed the covers off and hopped out of bed. He was nude and reached hurriedly for his jogging shorts. When he got his shorts on, he stretched on his toes, hands reaching for the ceiling. Then he yawned, shook his head and said, "Think I'll ease into the shower with Cindy. Be out in a second."

Ronnie picked up another one of Cindy's magazines. A while later Ronnie woke up from his dozing. Frank charged into the room, wet from the shower with Cindy's white robe on. The robe was way too short, stopping at his mid-thigh. Cindy poked her head from around the door. She tried slipping her arm around the door and snatching her robe but Frank jumped away.

"Frank, gimmie that robe!"

"Why you need it?"

"Ronnie's in there."

"Where?"

Ronnie waved his hands like he had nothing to do with what was happening.

"Fuck you, Frank!" Cindy said grinning, and ran in the room.

Ronnie, sitting on his beanbag, had a good view of their play-fighting. He had his eyes only on Cindy. She was as wet as Frank. Water ran from her thick, kinky hair down her face, to her breasts. He followed the lines of water past her breasts, and down farther. Cindy just about had the robe off Frank, so Ronnie quietly got up and went into the living room. Some time later Frank followed. He was dressed now in shorts, t-shirt and tennis shoes. But his clothes were cleaner than normal; Cindy had worked her domestic magic. She came out the room in her overalls, still hooking up the buckles as she frowned at Frank.

"I'll be back tonight," he said.

"What time?"

"Early."

He kissed Cindy goodbye, then ran back into the room to get his chess board and pieces.

"Be here around one, promise."

He gave a handsome grin and was out the door. Ronnie smiled to Cindy with a slightly bewildered look. He knew he was in the middle of something. Then Cindy said, "Frank's got a chess tournament early tomorrow morning."

"Yeah."

"Yeah."

"Oh."

"Try to get him to go home early."

"I'll do that."

"Sure Ron, in one ear and out the other."

Ronnie turned and walked out the door. He said bye as he shut it.

Frank was leaning on the tree by Ronnie's bike.

"Yeah Frank, still up to the old window hopping."

"Keeps me trim. She wants me on time, huh? Well, she can walk over my house in the late night. She can try to hop her butt through my window. And she can take all the chances I do."

They got on the bike, Ronnie kinda worrying about Frank leaning the wrong way. Then they took off down the hill.

"I DON'T KNOW WHAT'S HAPPENING with Frank," Garvy said agitatedly. He and Ronnie were in Garvy's Mama's kitchen, sitting around the table cutting cheese and eating it on crackers.

"He's up to something. He likes to be different, crazy and stuff."

"I don't know how he wants people to take this acting shit."

"You're not people, Garv. You're his partner."

"I know that, but you checked out his fingernails? Painted chestnut brown to go with his skin."

Ronnie smiled, paused and sliced a piece of cheese. Garvy reached in the icebox for the water jug, took a quick swallow and offered the jug to Ronnie.

"Naw, that's alright. But is that fingernail polish all that's fucking with you?"

"What's fucking with me is the type of shit he does. Deb was giving me and Frank a ride to the crib. I'm in the front talking to Deb. Man, I felt this hand rubbing me on my neck, I turn around the hand's gone. Cindy and Frank are sitting there smiling. So, I grin back and start talking to Deb again, playing the shit off. You know, Frank and Cindy always do that shit, it's cool...but then when Deb and I start talking again, I feel somebody's wet finger in my ear. I turned around and saw Frank pulling his hand back, so I swung on him. I wasn't really trying to hit him."

Garvy took another drink and walked into the next room, mumbling about putting a record on.

"You can talk Ron, I can hear you."

"But Garv, Frank always would play like that, what's so different about it now?"

Garvy started to say something but he lowered the stylus on to the record. The room was filled with the heavy boppin' of an old Lee Morgan album. Garvy sat back down. They had to talk louder over the music. It annoyed Ronnie but Garvy drummed and patted the table to it.

"But you know," Garvy said, "Frank always been open with touching. I don't mind, we all got ladies. I go with Deb and

Deb's Cindy's sister. Deb and I be fooling around in one room, Frank and Cindy in the next, so we could hug each other and wear flowers in our hair. Who gave a fuck? We had our women, now this shit!"

"Maybe he's getting tired of Cindy. He wants to get into something new."

"What you mean, Frank wants to be a pumpkin or something?"

"Believe what you want, I didn't say nothing about that. Frank got this other girlfriend Rita."

"Oh," Garvy said, "Frank's being deep again, reading that old encyclopedia of philosophy. So it's free love for you, me and everybody."

Ronnie looked grim and Garvy found himself watching his words. But he kept on talking.

"It would be cool if I could lay with Cindy. I thought about that pooh-bear. But how I'm gonna deal with Deb? It's cool when Frank puts his arm around me. Football players do that, my daddy does that, friends do that. But old weird-ass Frank, he gotta make something outta this shit. I see him trying this bullshit till I'm gonna have to talk to him about it." Garvy sat up in his chair and tried to imitate Frank's deep voice.

"'Who me, come on Garv, you're reading into this. Sure, I'm physical but it's not sexual unless you interpret it that way.' Yeah, Frank is gonna make me feel fucked up in the head."

Ronnie took his time to speak. It looked to Garvy like he was struggling with his words. "Sometimes you gotta find out what you can do and what you can't. You put yourself in a nutshell, you and Deb. Maybe you can make that work. But sometimes you gotta take chances."

Garvy stood up to put the water jug back in the icebox. The music was blowing loud. Garvy turned and started talking fast with words and his hands.

"I'll tell you what, I don't give a hot fuck about chances. I know Frank, he's good with women, they'll do for him. Now, he wants to see if he can get men to do for him."

The record finished playing. Garvy sat down, put his feet on the table. Then he jumped up to turn the record over.

THEY WERE IN THE PARK behind Cindy's house, sitting at a picnic table passing around a joint and cooling off their throats with wine that Cindy had smuggled from her house. It was a late fall evening. Cool breezes rustled through big broad leaves that covered the park grass. Frank and Cindy were wrapped up together in a blanket keeping warm.

Ronnie was on the other side of the table huddled against the cold.

"Come on over Ron and get under the blanket. Me and Cindy got more than enough room under here."

Frank stretched out the blanket to show Ronnie. Cindy nodded her agreement, so Ronnie moved over to their side of the table. Ronnie sat next to Frank and Frank handed him some blanket. Frank already had one arm around Cindy, so he put his other around Ronnie.

They talked for a while longer then Cindy got up to go and have dinner with her family. Frank didn't want her to go so soon.

"Cin, wait a while."

Frank walked over to Cindy and put his arms around her. Ronnie turned away like a good friend should while Frank and Cindy went to kissing. After a bit, Frank glanced over to Ronnie.

"Say fella, we'll be right back."

"The bushes?" Ronnie asked.

"Don't you realize the great worth of the lovers' privacy?"

"Well yeah, go ahead, leave me out here cold."

Cindy said, "You can come with us big boy."

"Naw, not my cup of tea."

Cindy and Frank got up, took the blanket and headed for the trees. A while later, Frank came back alone carrying the blanket.

"All through for the night?" Ronnie asked.

"Yeah, just had to walk the pooh-bear home."

"Sounds good."

"I'm gonna go see Rita tonight, though."

"How you gonna get there?"

Frank smiled smugly. "You're gonna give me a ride."

"Oh yeah, we'd better be getting on."

"There's no rush," Frank said looking away. The park lights came on in the distance. A breeze jumped up and Frank pulled the blanket around his shoulders. Then he reached to give Ronnie some of it. Ronnie mumbled his thanks and they finished what was left of the wine. Then Frank stretched and put his arm around Ronnie's shoulder. Ronnie tensed up. He didn't know what was gonna happen. He knew what could happen, and now he knew he didn't want it to.

"Frank, I gotta get on."

Frank drew his arm back. He didn't say anything. Ronnie got up tossing the blanket off and walked heavily towards the street. He was walking deaf. Trying not to hear Frank calling, if Frank would call.

IT WAS STILL EARLY. The big gym field was deserted. Garvy was sitting on the lawn stretching; his legs were open in a V. He'd touch his knee with his forehead twice, then go to the other leg. Then he'd grab his ankles and try to touch his forehead on the ground. This would squeeze the breath out of him and when he got it back he'd let out a loud "Fuuuuck!" and start at it again. After his glasses were fogged up enough so that he couldn't see his feet, he stood up to wipe them with his t-shirt. He wanted to find Ronnie. Ronnie had seen some girl and took the time out from stretching to walk her to her car. Garvy knew Ronnie's habits and so he decided to do some wind sprints instead of waiting. To make things interesting, he daydreamed himself into a halfback running those wind sprints. He charged back and forth on the field, high stepping the whole way. As he was making a fancy cut to the sidelines to avoid that shoestring tackle, a football bounced past him. He looked up and saw Ronnie trotting towards him.

"You get her number?" Garvy asked.

"Yeah, she lives around you."

"No shit, let's go around there."

"Maybe."

"You some piss-poor friend, holding out on me," Garvy said, picking up the football and throwing Ronnie a bullet. Ronnie ran over to the track; Garvy followed and they started a slow run.

"Ron, you wanna go over Frank's? He still got money from them chess games, could get some breakfast."

"I got some money. Stop bouncing, loosen up your arms. You gonna get tired running like that."

"I didn't know that, shit."

Garvy tried to run smoother but quit when Ronnie turned his head.

"Well, you wanna go around there?" Garvy asked again.

"Naw."

"I guess you and Frank had some falling out."

"Yeah, I guess."

"You gonna see him again?"

"I don't know. Probably."

"What happened?" Garvy asked.

"What happened?" Ronnie repeated the question like he was considering it.

"Yeah, what went on, between you and Frank?"

"Nothing much."

"Something happened, dog! Tell me!" Garvy started to chase Ron.

But because he was already tired from jogging, he changed his mind quick enough. Ronnie grinned at Garvy being nosy.

"Nothing happened, man!" Ronnie tried to look pestered but he ended up grinning at his lie. Garvy running alongside, said "Yeah." He had an idea about what happened. It was alright that Ronnie wouldn't tell him. He would want to hear too many details.

Homebreaker

GUMBO CREPT QUIETLY through the hall that led to the back door. He didn't want to wake his father who was asleep at the kitchen table. Actually, his father was drunk and wasn't likely to wake up, but the situation still required secrecy. Rita, Dinky's wife, was waiting for him in the alley. Gumbo reached the back door and managed to open it and get through without making too much noise. He walked through the small backyard onto his father's newly-built enclosed patio. (The older fellas in the neighborhood didn't think too much of it since it leaked.) And through the patio into the alley, where he saw Rita waiting on him.

"You gonna get me high?" she asked, with her hands on her hips, sounding more like she was demanding, than asking a question.

"Do me, I'll do you." Gumbo said and took her hand and led her on to the patio. They sat down on the couch across from the gas fireplace. Gumbo had turned it on before he sat down and now it was getting warm and comfortable inside the airy patio. Gumbo reached under the couch and pulled out a shoe box top, which had his rolling papers and a plastic bag with his dope. By moonlight Gumbo managed to roll three joints. The whole while Rita was silent, she never said much anyway, but this time she was quiet like she was thinking.

"Dinky knows I'm coming over here."

"Yeah?"

"He ain't said nothing but he knows."

"You wanna stop coming?"

"No, but he might hit me or something."

"Fuck him, you said you was gonna divorce his ass. All that niggah ever did for you was give you that baby."

Gumbo lit a joint and passed it to her. He let her smoke it down, she tried to pass it back to him but he waved it away. He reached behind her and untied her halter blouse, kissing her breasts and neck.

"Gumbo, stop."

He kept at it and was able to slip off her skirt, he knew she wanted him to, otherwise she wouldn't have worn a skirt. (It was almost too hard to get a girl out of a pair of tight jeans if she didn't want you to.)

"Let's smoke another joint first?" she asked.

Gumbo lit another one, took a few quick hits and did as before, let her finish it up. Gumbo didn't have to rush, Rita liked to stay out late, her mama didn't care. Dinky cared, but he didn't live with Rita, he lived a few blocks away with his mama, and since Rita's mama didn't like him, he didn't come over too often. They were married so the baby could have a name, but they didn't get along well. When she would cook oatmeal for the baby, Dinky would eat it. And when he would try to beat her up, she would grab for his privates and claw at his face.

Gumbo left to use the patio bathroom. (He liked that best about the patio, a backyard bathroom. But he liked the built-in barbeque pit, too.)

When he came back, Rita was stretched out on the couch, she had only her panties on, but she was using her skirt to cover herself with. He knelt to kiss her and tossed the skirt to the floor.

Dinky didn't want to disturb Mr. Villabino by knocking on the door at one in the morning.

He knew Rita was in there with Gumbo, everybody knew. Gumbo loved to tell his secrets. Dinky didn't care too much, Rita's mama wouldn't let her give any money to him and all she would cook when he was around was oatmeal.

He didn't care about sleeping with her after the baby. He just wished that everybody would stop bugging him about Rita and Gumbo. Even his brother Junior was telling him to do something. (He didn't know how Junior could have found out, being in jail and everything.) Another thing was why she wanted to sleep with Gumbo, how could it even work, it was like he had a beach ball wrapped around his mid-section. He figured she must have to get on top or something, and thinking about how they could work it out made him even madder. Dinky decided he would go around to the backyard and sneak up to Gumbo's window and see if they were at it.

When Gumbo heard somebody opening the gate he told Rita to be quiet, then quickly put on his pants and opened the sliding door, and went outside to see. He saw a very skinny guy peeking into his window. At first he thought it was somebody who wanted to buy a joint, but this guy wasn't tapping at the window to wake him up, he was peeking, looking to see something.

"Whatcha doing at my window?!" The guy turned around at Gumbo's question. Then Gumbo could see that it was Dinky.

"Where's Rita?"

"Rita?"

"My wife."

"Your wife, you married?"

"She's over."

"You oughta go home, she's probably there waiting on you."

"Where she at, Gumbo!" Gumbo heard the sliding glass window open behind him; he could feel Rita standing at his side.

"I'm going home Gumbo."

"You gonna get your ass kicked when you get there," Dinky said.

Rita didn't say anything, she followed Dinky out of the yard. But before they got through the gate, Dinky slapped her on the back of the head. Gumbo ran around to the front yard. Dinky and Rita were standing on the edge of his lawn almost in the street. Dinky didn't seem too interested in hitting her. He was waving his arms and shouting, which looked like it was giving him a lot of satisfaction.

"Why with Gumbo! What that fat boy do for you?"

"You ain't my husband, I'm gonna divorce your stupid ass!"

"What does he do?"

"I ain't answering you!"

Then Dinky saw Gumbo standing by his porch without shoes or shirt, watching him argue with Rita. Dinky walked over to Gumbo like he wanted to fight, got halfway there and thought better of it. (Gumbo outweighed him by more than a hundred pounds.)

"Yeah, you fat motherfucka, fucking my wife, but you a dickless dog, can't find none of your own!"

One thing Dinky was sure of, he could outrun Gumbo. And Gumbo knew it didn't make much sense to try and catch Dinky, they stared at each other for a long while.

"Walk me home, Dinky," Rita said.

"What?" Dinky wouldn't turn from trying to stare Gumbo down.

"Walk me home!"

Rita had her hands on her hips again, looking impatient. Dinky finally turned away from Gumbo.

"I'll talk to your fat ass later!" Dinky said, waving his finger at Gumbo.

Gumbo watched them walk off, Dinky slightly behind Rita, trying to keep pace with her small quick steps. Gumbo wondered if Dinky was going to sweet talk his way into spending the night at Rita's.

Making the Move

GARVY WAS WATCHING the late news when the phone rang. After putting his snacks aside and wriggling out of the recliner, he had to run to get it by the fourth ring.

"Hi Garvy! What you're doing?"

Garvy was surprised, it was Debra. "Where you're calling from Debra, I thought school was still in at San Diego."

"It is, I'm calling from my dorm room."

Garvy was more surprised, a long-distance call.

"What's happening Debra, you up to no good at school?"

"No, I'm just studying hard and getting ready for finals."

"So, you'll be home pretty soon?"

"In a week or two."

"Well, I got these tickets to see Dexter Gordon, if you wanna go."

"I don't know Garv, if I'm around then."

"It's the 25th of March, that's two weeks."

"I'm going up to San Francisco with some friends. So, I don't know when I'll be in L.A."

"Oh, okay." Garvy paused for a moment, "But if you change your mind…"

"Thanks Garv. Garv, I've got a huge favor to ask you. My mama and Cindy are having a big fight over our good friend Frank. I was just wondering if you could talk to Frank."

"Talk to Frank, what can I talk to Frank about?"

"Well, Garv, the whole thing is about Frank's window hopping. He doesn't do that anymore."

"So what's the deal, your mama wants Frank to start hopping through Cindy's window again?"

"Oh Garvy, my mama and Cindy are fighting because Frank won't leave. He's staying in her room. He's moved in."

Garvy smiled, he'd been trying to catch up to Frank lately. He was starting to wonder where Frank was spending his time.

"Yeah, I'll talk to him, your mama is gonna try to throw him in jail or something?"

"I don't know what my mama is gonna do, but I'm getting awful mad at Frank and Cindy."

"Well, I'll talk to him."

"Thanks Garv, but you oughta know that my mama thinks Frank's on something."

"On what?"

"My mama thinks it's Angel Dust or something like that. But I don't know what it is."

"Frank's not on anything." Garvy knew that the only thing Frank messed around with was weed and wine unless he was playing chess, then it was whites. Frank liked to stay up all night playing chess. Garvy guessed coffee didn't do anything for him or that he got tired of pissing every half hour.

"If he's not, he's acting pretty weird then, not wanting to leave."

"Well, you know, free room and board."

"Are you going to talk to him, Garvy?"

"I'll talk to him."

"Thanks Garv. So, I'll be seeing you in a while."

"Okay, take it easy, bye."

Garvy hung up and decided to steal one of his brother's beers.

He couldn't believe that. What a bitch, he thought. He opened the refrigerator and cursed at the milk in front of the beer. He cursed at the jello for the same reason. He ripped apart the six pack, cursing Debra with every pull. He thought about how she wouldn't write him, wouldn't call, and now because of her stupid homicidal family, she was getting in touch with him for a favor. And what was he supposed to talk to Frank about? Frank at least came around his place looking to buy a pizza with him, not to ask him a favor, like kick his partner out of a good thing. It was true that he and Frank couldn't talk much about things, but they could still get along. Debra sure didn't act like his friend, she was asking too much of him. And besides she wouldn't even go out with him.

GARVY STOOD IN FRONT OF DEBRA'S HOUSE, but since Debra was still away, walking up to the house didn't cause him to feel uneasy or make him nervous. Without Debra the house was defanged. He rang the doorbell. Brenda opened the door, Garvy noticed how big Debra's youngest sister was getting. She was filling out but she still had that dumb look in her eye and no matter how shapely she got, she was still going to be unattractive to him.

"Debra's not here," she said quickly.

"I know that Brenda, is Cindy here?"

"Yeah…"

"Well go tell her I'm here, Brenda."

Brenda crossed the short distance to Cindy's bedroom and knocked on the door. Cindy yelled from her bedroom.

"What!"

"Garvy's here."

There was no response. Garvy started to rub his hands on his shirt. He felt like two-week-old trash. Brenda walked in the den to watch her Saturday morning cartoons. He decided to have a seat and unwrap some candies on the coffee table. He didn't want to eat any, his stomach was too nervous, so he sniffed them. After sniffing through the green, orange and yellow candies, he realized that jellied sugar candy doesn't have much of a smell. Then Cindy opened the door, grinned at him and waved him into the room. Garvy walked into her small bedroom and saw Frank nicely tucked in Cindy's bed reading a book. Cindy left them to cook breakfast. Frank gave Garvy a knowing smile, but Garvy had no idea what they were both supposed to know. Garvy thought he should be on guard, he sat down in the easy chair in the corner.

"Just relaxing on a late Saturday morning, eh Frank?"

"Yeah, I'm resting up, big chess tournament last night. I have one tomorrow too, so I'm just relaxing."

"Well, you're gonna lay dead today?"

"Yeah, I think I need this rest."

It was annoying Garvy that Frank wouldn't sit up in the bed. He was lying back with just his head propped, he was in the same position that he'd been reading his book in, except now he had his head turned to look at Garvy. It bothered him more that Frank had his book opened and resting on his stomach as if to threaten Garvy about being too boring. Garvy thought he might as well get to the point.

"Well, when you're ready to go I'll walk with you."

"I'm not going for a while."

"I thought you wanted to crash."

"I can do that fine here," Frank said.

Debra was right, Garvy thought, Frank was staying put.

"Don't you think you oughta be gone when Mrs. Jameson gets back?"

"Why?"

Garvy paused for a second. "Because she's having the house fumigated."

Frank sat up in bed. "Cindy didn't tell me about that. I'll have to go. Throw me my shorts."

Frank dressed hurriedly and looked anxious about leaving. It's the twenty games of chess a day that fucked him up, Garvy thought. Garvy decided to search through Cindy's bookcase and give Frank privacy to dress even if he didn't want it. Frank moved over to the easy chair that Garvy abandoned.

"Garv, you think this could be a ploy. When did Mrs. Jameson tell you about getting the house gassed? I bet she's trying to trick me to get me out of here."

Frank was so mad at Mrs. Jameson that he threw himself hard into the easy chair. He looked thoughtful for a moment, then grimaced and twisted up in a knot. He started cursing loudly and rocking back and forth in the chair. Cindy ran into the room and slammed the door shut so that Brenda couldn't follow.

"Frank! What's wrong?!" Cindy yelled.

"I sat on my nuts," he said in a low voice.

"Want me to get some hot water?" Cindy said.

"What am I gonna do with hot water? I just want to sit here."

Garvy was content to watch Frank moaning and Cindy fretting but he heard Mrs. Jameson pull up. Whatever was going to happen with Mrs. Jameson and Frank, Garvy didn't want to be there. But she was heading for the door, he couldn't get out unseen, so he figured it was better to stay put.

"Do you think I could get a ride home?" Frank asked Cindy. "I think I'm pretty swollen."

He tried to stand but it hurt too much, so he gently lowered himself back in the chair.

"I'll ask my mother if I can use the car."

The front door opened, Mrs. Jameson was in the house. Garvy was sure there was going to be a scene. Cindy didn't seem very aware of that, she ran straight to her mother to get permission to use the car.

"Mama, Frank hurt himself, you've got to let me use the car to get him to the hospital."

Mrs. Jameson dirty-eyed her daughter, she was tired from shopping and Cindy didn't even help her with the bags. And that damn Frank was still in the house.

"You better tell your boyfriend to get the bus. He's not setting his ass in my car."

"Mama, he's sick. I've got to take him."

"Tell him you'll take him on your back," replied Mrs. Jameson.

Cindy leaned forward and snatched her mother's purse off her shoulder and headed for the front door. She yelled for Frank and went outside. Mrs. Jameson was so astonished, she just

watched Cindy walk out the door with Frank hobbling behind
her. Garvy figured Mrs. Jameson was going to run out the house,
hog-tie her daughter, and shoot Frank. But she didn't, she sat
down by the telephone, lit a cigarette and listened to her car
being driven away. Garvy thought that Mrs. Jameson didn't know
he was there, but without looking up she started talking to him.

"Could you believe that, my daughter and her boyfriend
steal my car and now I'm going to have to bring the police into
this."

Garvy didn't say anything, he tried to look sincere and sym-
pathetic.

"It's that goddamn Frank's fault. Well, his aunt will have to
get him out of jail," she said.

Garvy thought he should say something to keep Mrs.
Jameson from reporting her car being stolen but nothing came
to mind so he kept quiet.

"Garvy, did Frank really hurt himself?"

"Yes, he twisted something."

"Oh, good for him. Do you know he won't go home? He
thinks he lives here. I didn't mind too much them sleeping
together, trying to keep them from doing that is like trying to
keep the white off rice. But Frank moving in...I'm gonna get
him out of this house, and if Cindy wants to go with him, fine."

Mrs. Jameson started dialing. Garvy got up and left.

Garvy spent the rest of the day at home wondering what
had happened. He waited around hovering over the telephone,
he didn't know who was going to call, or if anybody was going to
call and tell him what had happened. But Garvy had to know, so
he kept watch over the telephone and was finally rewarded.

"Garvy! I'm downtown across from city hall."

"What're you doing there, Frank?"

"The police station is down the street, I walked here from
there."

"You were at the police station?"

"Yeah, they thought I was crazy when I told them how I

was hurt. They wouldn't believe me until one of them decided to get the jail doctor to see how swollen I was."

"They let you go when they saw you were sick?"

"Yeah, but trying to convince them to get a doctor and then finding the guy took quite a while. Hell, they took so much time my swelling went down."

"It's good that you're better, tell me when you get home, then we'll go get something to eat."

"Garvy I'm calling to get a ride."

"Alright man, I'll pick you up, I know where it is."

"Thanks Garv."

The drive downtown didn't take that long and would have been short if Garvy had got off at the right exit. Garvy saw Frank standing on the corner, next to the phone booth. Garvy pulled over.

"Get in brother," Garvy said to Frank.

Frank hopped in eagerly from the cold night air.

"Thanks for the ride, Garv. I got some money, I'll buy us a pizza, if we can find a pizza place open."

"Yeah, sounds like a thing to do," Garvy said.

"Damn Garv, it was a weird evening. I don't know exactly what happened about those police picking me and Cindy up, but I figured Mrs. Jameson wasn't mad at Cindy anymore, so she told the police that I put Cindy up to stealing her car. But since I wasn't driving, just sitting there moaning, they let me go after keeping me five or six hours. The police told me not to come near Mrs. Jameson's house, something about grand theft auto. They said I got off easy but next time..."

"Police always talking about next time. You're going around there again?"

"Naw, not till everything blows over. I'm gonna stay with my brother in Long Beach, then I can get serious about chess. Get away from girls, improve my game."

"Good idea," Garvy said nodding his head earnestly.

Face

AT THE POOL HALL, Gumbo changed his mind about going inside. He wanted to go in, but the pool hall's weathered door that was shut during business hours, and the windows that were caked with dirt, and especially the loud argument that was going on inside, made him hesitate. He turned from the pool hall, acting nonchalant as if somebody was watching him change his plans. He glanced around the street, finally looking toward the pawnshop and the fried chicken stand next to it. Gumbo decided to run across to the fried chicken stand. He stood in line and waited to place his order. He was smelling the fried chicken and getting an appetite when he felt an arm wrap around his shoulders. It was Mad Tony.

"Gumbo! Gum-bo! Gumm-Boo! My boy, one of my boys! Get down Gumbo!"

Tony squeezed Gumbo as hard as he could. Gumbo expected this and pushed himself free from Mad Tony's embrace.

"What's up, Tony?"

"Mad T, call me Mad T, that's a cool name, ain't it? Short, too. Can say it real quick, Mad T, Mad T, see?"

"Alright Tony, I'll call you Mad T."

Mad T was pretty big, and he didn't mind fighting. Gumbo tried to humor him most of the time.

"Buy me some chicken," Mad T said.

"Buy your own."

"Come on, Gumbo, buy T some chicken."

T wrapped his arms around Gumbo again.

"Let go, you poor ass niggah. I'll buy you a piece."

"Yeah," T let go with one of his arms but still kept one arm around Gumbo in a manly fashion.

Gumbo placed his order and they waited for it while sitting

on top of a happy-looking plastic picnic table. Gumbo sat quietly, hoping T wouldn't want to start a conversation.

"What you up to Gumbo? If you ain't doing nothing, let's go over to your house and get high and watch TV. The TV over my house broke and my daddy think I done it so he won't get it fixed."

"I'm not going home."

"That's cool, whatever, I'll hang with you. It ain't like I got a whole lot to do, I just got out of the place a couple of months ago, that's why I got on these prison shoes, but pretty soon I'm gonna be styling."

They called Gumbo's number at the little pick-up window. Gumbo got his food and went back to the picnic table. He handed T a drumstick, then he turned his back on T and started eating his food. Gumbo could eat quick so he finished a drumstick and a wing before T could start worrying him about another piece.

"I'm gonna go shoot some pool," Gumbo said.

"Shoot pool, huh? Yeah, I got some cash. Let's do that."

"You got cash, buy your own chicken! And give me back my sixty-five cents, acting like your ass ain't got money!"

Mad T stood up and laughed. "I'll shoot you for it," he said. They finished eating and walked back to the pool hall. Gumbo let Mad T take the lead. The pool hall's closed door hardly slowed Mad T. He stepped in quickly. Gumbo had to hurry to keep up with him. The inside of the pool hall was dark and dank and smelled of urine. The floor looked uneven; his father would probably say the concrete wasn't mixed enough so it dried wrong. The three pool tables had thin, flat pieces of wood under their legs to level them out.

Mad T and Gumbo stopped at a pool table that had a crowd of people hanging around it. Two fellas were cooly and intently shooting a game. They were both thin, hard-looking types, who dressed in somber colors. Gumbo admired how they would squat and squint at the way their shot was lining up. He was in the presence of sharks. Gumbo was captivated by the pool players and he wanted to watch the sharks put on a show. They were so tense, never saying a word, unless they were calling a shot, and then they talked hurriedly, snapping off the tail end of their words. The game went on for some time, until one of the sharks called a pocket and knocked the eight ball into it, then without smiling he nodded to his opponent and they left the pool hall. Gumbo figured they were playing for money and didn't want to show cash with so many people around. Gumbo enjoyed their mysterious and deliberate manner. Now he was ready to play a game. Mad Tony, who looked bored, nodded his agreement. The pool hall door opened, and a tall, fat guy with a black trench coat (it was 85 degrees outside) came into the room. It was Jackie Engine. Gumbo looked for a back exit, he was trapped. A few of Jackie Engine's friends followed him into the pool hall. They sat in the row of seats by the far wall of the room. Jackie leaned back in his chair and looked around the room. He stopped at Gumbo. Gumbo turned to Mad T.

"I'm gonna split."

T was talking to one of the pool players. It looked as though he was going to be a long time. Gumbo walked toward the door without looking back. He was trying not to look in Jackie Engine's direction, but he heard Jackie get up and walk toward him. He grabbed Gumbo by the arm.

"What's up, fat boy, I need you to help me out. I need some cash," he said in a low voice.

"I ain't got no cash."

Jackie screwed his lip up at Gumbo, then slapped him on the face. Gumbo turned red. He rubbed his face and looked at Jackie.

"Don't talk shit to me, Gumbo."

Gumbo reached down into his sock and pulled out a roll of bills and handed them to Jackie. Jackie snatched it out of his hand.

"Get outta here, fat boy."

Gumbo turned to walk out and saw that most of the people in the pool hall were looking at him. He walked home quickly, but he didn't know what he was going to do when he got there.

When Gumbo got home he decided he didn't want to go right in. He lay on his porch steps and closed his eyes. What just happened had his stomach burning. He lay there and thought about what kind of fool he was. One hundred and twenty-five dollars, his pay for two weeks' work, was in the pocket of Jackie Engine, and that wasn't the bad part. The bad part was that everybody in the pool hall had seen him get robbed. This was some sad, sorry shit. Why the fuck did that nasty niggah scare him like that? It didn't make no sense. He let him slap him too; he should have brought Jackie home to screw his sister, that was about the only thing Jackie hadn't done. This just about killed his respectability in the neighborhood. Gumbo could handle dodging Jackie, and even getting his money taken when he couldn't dodge him. But it was sort of private and discreet, now it was public knowledge—he was the pussy that got took. Gumbo stood up and went into his house. He called his sister's name a few times but she didn't answer. He went into his parent's bedroom. The door was locked. He leaned back and kicked it. It didn't open. He stood a few feet back and charged into the door. He jarred his teeth but the door didn't give. He walked to the kitchen and came back with an ice pick. He stuck it into the lock and jiggled it around till something gave and the door opened. His parents' room was a mess. Clothes were tossed everywhere. Now he knew why they kept the door locked. He searched through their dresser until he found his father's .22. He checked to see if it was loaded. It was. The doorbell rang. He left the room to answer it. He opened the door. It was Mad Tony.

"Gumbo, what's up man? That was some raw shit. Jackie hitting you up like that. You shoulda fucked him up when he slapped you. Shit, I was gonna get into his ass but it happened too fast. You better lay dead for a while, he said he still gonna fuck you up, unless you give him some more cash."

Gumbo stood very still and looked at Mad Tony through the screen door.

"Jackie still up there?"

"Yeah, he was when I left."

"Tell him I got something for him."

"What you got?"

"Something he can suck on."

Gumbo took the gun out of his pocket and showed it to Tony.

"Tell him to stay there so I can shoot him."

Mad Tony's eyes got big, he nodded and walked quickly off the porch.

After Mad Tony left, Gumbo closed the door and decided to do some drinking. He got his Mama's rum out of the liquor cabinet and went into the kitchen and tried to find something to mix it with. The only thing he could find was some left-over lime Kool-aid. He drank it quickly, it didn't taste too good. He left his house and started the walk to the pool hall. He tried to keep himself calm but it wasn't working. He didn't know what he was going to say to Jackie. He knew he was going to demand his money back and if Jackie decided to jump bad, he was going to shoot him. The niggah deserved it. Treat him like some stupid bitch he could slap and rob, he oughta just shot him on the spot. Yeah, the punk needed to be dead. Gumbo was almost up to the pool hall. Now he was worked up into a fit. He just wanted to shoot Jackie. He opened the pool hall door and walked in. Most of the crowd was gone but Mad Tony was still there. He walked over to Gumbo, looking excited.

"Gumbo! Jackie Engine just left. Said he's gonna go get his shit!"

"You told him what I said?"

"Yeah, I think you scared him, but he still said you wasn't shit. Said, if he sees you, he's gonna hurt you for real."

"Fuck him, I'll go around to his house."

Gumbo turned and walked out of the pool hall, Mad Tony

followed him. Something was happening to him. He really did want to shoot Jackie. They walked around the corner and up the street to Jackie Engine's. Gumbo looked at the small, nicely kept house with the two palm trees out front. He felt the gun in his pocket and started for the front door.

"Whatcha gonna do, Gumbo, walk up to his house?"

Gumbo didn't answer. He continued walking toward the door. Mad Tony called him from the sidewalk, "You wanna get killed or something?"

"I don't know," Gumbo said, without looking back. He knocked on the door. A dark, fat lady opened it. She looked sweaty and tired. Gumbo guessed she had been doing housework. She curled her lip at Gumbo as she wiped her hands on her apron.

"What do you want? I told Jackie about letting his hoodlum friends knock at the door. Take your ass out of here! That thug son of mine ain't home. Go!" Gumbo found himself walking off the porch before thinking about it. Mad Tony was laughing at him.

"Jackie and his mama don't get along too well."

"You shoulda told me."

Gumbo decided to go back home. Then he thought Jackie could be waiting for him and that he would have to go through the alley. He noticed Mad Tony was following at his heels. Gumbo summoned his tact.

"Mad T, I'm gonna go home and lay dead. I'll catch up with you later on tonight."

Mad Tony nodded, "I'll keep an eye open, if I see something I'll get back to you."

He gave Gumbo a manly hug that lingered a few moments too long for Gumbo, and then walked off in the opposite direction. Gumbo made good time through the alley. He opened the back gate and hurried through his backyard into his house. Gumbo was lying down in his bed in a light sleep when his father banged on his bedroom door and woke him up. He rolled out of bed and opened the door. His father stood in the doorway and scowled at him as he climbed back into bed.

"Boy, you got my gun!"

"Gun? I ain't got no gun."

Mr. Villabino shook his finger at Gumbo and walked into the room and slammed the door shut.

"Boy, didn't I say don't lie to me."

"How am I lying?"

"Somebody broke the lock on my door and that was you. Don't lie to me, Gumbo!"

"Look, I ain't got no gun, you can forget that."

"I can forget it, yeah. Sure boy, I can forget your ass, with my foot up it."

Mr. Villabino grabbed the handle of Gumbo's dresser and pulled the top drawer out and flung Gumbo's watch and two screw drivers, with other odds and ends in the drawer, at his son. Gumbo shielded his head behind his arms.

"Why you wanna fuck with me!" Gumbo shouted.

Mr. Villabino grabbed the second drawer, and this time threw the whole drawer at Gumbo. It hit him on the knee. He got out of bed fast, rubbing his knee. His father finished searching the rest of the drawers.

"I don't got your gun!" Gumbo shouted.

His father stopped kicking through the clothes he had tossed on the floor.

"I want that gun," Mr. Villabino said, scowling, and walked out.

Gumbo started picking up his stuff that his father had scattered around the room. He knew things were going to get a lot worse if he didn't give the gun back. Gumbo dressed quickly and got out of the house unseen by his father. He went outside onto the patio, went to the couch and lifted the cushions and picked up the gun and pushed it deep into his pocket. He decided to visit Garvy and show him his piece.

Garvy came out of the house with a beer for Gumbo. He

didn't offer Gumbo any of the pork skins he had covered with hot sauce till he piled up a good amount on his napkin. Gumbo, who was lying on the steps, sat up.

"Take them all for yourself, huh?"

Garvy cut his eyes at Gumbo. "I paid for them, I do what I want with them."

"That's why you ass is so fat."

"You want some or not?"

Gumbo snatched the bag from him. He looked inside and was happy a fair amount remained.

"So you reached in your sock for your cash?"

"The niggah had me like a snake. I thought he was gonna kill me, he had his boys there, too."

"What you gonna do?"

"I wanna shoot him."

Gumbo paused and looked down the street. He saw Mad Tony coming. Garvy looked too.

"Hey, here comes your weird partner," Garvy said.

Mad Tony walked up to the porch, strutting. He had his neck out and his shoulders back, bobbing his head to a beat. He nodded to both of them when he arrived at the porch. He sat next to Garvy and put his arm around him and tried to coax a handshake. Garvy took his hand without much enthusiasm. This didn't deter Tony. He put his other arm around Garvy and hugged tightly. Garvy shook him off.

"Don't touch me!" Garvy shouted.

"What?" Tony said, surprised.

"Don't touch me!"

"What's he talking about, Gumbo?"

"I don't know, he don't want you touching him."

Mad Tony stood up and went toward Garvy. Garvy stepped back.

"Why you want to be like that, Garv. I'm your partner from way back. It ain't cool to dog out your partners."

Garvy sat down on the porch again. Mad Tony moved to sit next to him.

"Don't sit next to me," Garvy said.

"Man, I thought we were partners. We go way back."

"Just don't sit next to me."

Mad Tony sat next to Gumbo. He put his arm around Gumbo and smiled.

"Gumbo and me, we're partners, from way back."

Garvy stood up and went into the house. Gumbo crossed over to where Garvy was sitting.

"Jackie's down the street. He was talking about coming down to look for you," Mad Tony said.

"When he said that?"

"Right before I came down here."

"He had any of his boys with him?"

"Bobby and Big Humbug."

"I'll be back. I'm gonna use Garvy's head."

Garvy's front door was unlocked. Gumbo walked in, locked the door and found Garvy in the kitchen cooking a hamburger.

"I'm gonna split. Mad Tony told me Jackie got his boys and is looking out for me."

"Cutting through the alley?"

"Yeah."

"I'll walk with you."

Garvy turned off the hamburger and they left out the back door. Garvy pushed aside his dog and they walked through the alley gate. Gumbo's house was right across the alley about three houses down. Gumbo opened the gate and was about halfway through when he turned back into the yard.

"Jackie and his boys are waiting by my gate," he whispered.

Gumbo picked up a crate and placed it next to the fence. Gumbo waved for Garvy to be quiet. Jackie and his two boys were standing where Gumbo wouldn't be able to see them coming out of his gate, but from Garvy's yard, they were out in the open. Garvy got a crate and stood next to Gumbo. Gumbo pulled his father's gun out, held it with two hands, and rested it on the width of the cement fence. He aimed at Jackie who was standing in the center. Gumbo sucked in his breath and there was a loud bang. Jackie spun around, smacked against the fence and fell to the ground. Gumbo fired again but missed him. Bobby and Big Humbug took off running. Jackie was lying face down, but moving a little bit. Gumbo and Garvy watched for a while, then hopped off the crates.

"He's not dead," Gumbo said.

"So what! You crazy bitch, shooting him from my yard. I don't even know your ass. Get the fuck out of my yard!"

"Give me a ride to the beach."

"Fuck you."

Both of them walked quickly into Garvy's house.

"Drive me to the beach. I wanna throw the gun into the ocean."

"Boy, you better walk."

"Who you calling?"

"The paramedics. Somebody got to pick him up."

"You ain't gonna give me a ride?"

"No."

"I want to ditch the gun."

"Do it, but first get out of my house."

Garvy started talking on the phone. Gumbo watched him for a while, then left. He didn't walk around the corner to his house where Jackie was lying. He knew there would be a crowd now. He walked up the street till he was six blocks away. He crossed into an alley and stuck the gun deep into a trash can. He walked home slowly, taking his time and thinking about his situation. He stopped and ordered a hamburger at the chinese food bowling alley. He gobbled it down and went to the telephone and made a call.

His Mama answered. "Hi Ma, did Mary call?"

"Boy, where you at! All types of big commotion is going on around here. Somebody shot that Jackie Engine boy."

"Yeah, how long ago?"

"Not too long ago. Police are all over the neighborhood."

"He's bad?"

"Not too bad. Jeanie May's little girl found him, said he was trying to crawl but couldn't get too far. She got her daddy and they wrapped him up in blankets till the ambulance came."

"Mama. I been with Garvy all day, at the park."

"Come home to eat."

"Maybe later."

"Come on, boy."

"I'll be there."

But he knew he wasn't. He was going to spend the next few days with his Aunt Mary.

A few days later Gumbo came back home. His father was in the kitchen reading the paper. As Gumbo was walking past him, his father grabbed his arm.

"Boy, where is that gun?"

"I told you I ain't got no gun."

"You don't, huh, well how that boy got shot?"

"I don't know nothing about that."

"Nobody is no fool, Gumbo."

Gumbo didn't say anything.

"Just be glad boy, the lord gave you a lotta luck for your lack of brains."

Gumbo turned to leave. His father raised his voice and stopped him.

"That boy wasn't hurt too bad. Nobody saw you, you lucky boy."

"Yeah, some lucky," Gumbo said.

He went into his bedroom. He locked the door and called Mad Tony.

"Tony, what's up?"

"You got him! Serves the punk right."

"Yeah."

"I heard Jackie is leaving to Texas for a while, his Mama is sending him there to get well, away from niggahs."

Gumbo sat on the bed and sighed.

"Thought that would make you happy. But Jackie's boys are out after you. Stay low. You know them Crips stick together."

"Yeah, I gotta go eat. I'll check with you."

Gumbo hung up without waiting for Tony's goodbye. Things were finally starting to calm down, he hoped.

Loose Ends

FRANK WAS READING HIS CHESS BOOK. He was near-sighted, so he held the book close to his face and moved his chess pieces with his other hand. He practiced being a dramatic and dynamic mover of his pieces; he figured any edge in a game was worth trying for, even if it meant knocking the chair over and standing up to make a move that he could have made sitting down. He decided he would quit studying at three and do some reading, then go for a walk up the La Brea hill. The phone rang. Frank had developed the habit of not answering the phone, but everybody was asleep.

"Yes," he said.

"Frank, you still stay up late playing chess?"

"Cindy?"

"Forgot my voice, huh, Frank?"

"No."

"Do you feel like walking?"

"Yeah."

"Come on over, the window will be open."

"All right," he said, and hung up.

He looked at his chess board for a while. He hadn't seen her for a month or two; she went away to college, now she was back. What bothered him was how easy it was for her to pick up and leave. He knew she was planning to go, it was the timing that pissed him off. He had thought she was still there when he phoned after a respectable absence, and Mrs. Jameson had told him with satisfaction that Cindy had gone away to college, and there wasn't any reason for him to call there anymore. He wanted to ask her why the fuck would he call if Cindy wasn't there.

Frank passed Cindy's mama's car, and stopped to rip the antenna off. He twirled it, then sliced and jabbed the air and finally tossed it aside. He walked onto the lawn and took his shirt off and tossed it on the lawn. He did the same with his shorts, and lay naked in her front yard. Then he went to Cindy's window and tapped. He waited like a crazy man. Frank saw a pair of hands opening the window and felt relieved. He jumped, grabbed the windowsill and pulled himself up, and as usual, had to struggle to get in. Inside he could barely make out Cindy kneeling on the bed, looking at him. One thing he could see was that her hair wasn't long anymore, it was cut into a short natural. He bent forward to kiss her, but hugged her instead.

"Frank, you got grass sticking all over you."

Frank kissed her. At first she was reluctant about the grass, but he was able to get things started. Afterward, he was ready to sleep.

"Frank, you oughta leave, my mama is gonna be getting up soon."

"So, you still let her check up on you?"

"Look, I don't wanta go through the changes. I'm just asking you to leave before she wakes up."

"Boy, you're a straight-out responsible woman. College must do wonders."

"Just come back later in the day. I'm not doing anything. We can go to the beach."

"Sure, anything to tickle your fancy. How about doing me a favor and getting my clothes off the lawn."

"Okay, but you oughta get off those nature boy trips. Somebody might try to plug you, thinking you're a pervert."

"Hey, I might even enjoy that. Go get my stuff."

Frank watched her as she got out of bed and put on a flannel gown. His eyes started to water. He sat up in the bed and wrapped his arms around his knees and rocked. He was amazed at how much he hated her. After she left to go outside he followed her, tiptoeing naked through the house, the chance of little Brenda out of bed for water or the bathroom, maybe even surprising Mrs. Jameson, made him so excited that he felt jittery.

He looked out the door and saw Cindy with his clothes bundled under her arm, still searching the lawn to make sure she had everything. Frank waited till she noticed him, then as she moved toward him, gesturing for him to be quiet, he shut and locked the door. He went back to the bedroom and hopped out the window. After brushing some thorns off his feet he walked around to the porch where Cindy was knocking lightly at the door.

"Hi Cin," Frank said, startling her.

"You locked us out the house."

"Yep."

"Why?"

"I don't know, wanted some air."

"I can't get in."

"Why you want to? You're out here with me."

"I don't want to be out here with your silly ass. I want to be in the house."

Frank walked onto the porch and took his shorts from her, but didn't put them on. He put his hands around her waist.

"Missed you," he said and kissed her hard on the mouth. He lifted her flannel gown.

"Let's sit down," he said.

They did. Cindy adjusted her gown but Frank was pulling it up soon as they were sitting.

"My butt is cold," Cindy said.

Frank slid his shorts under her. He pushed her back till she was lying on the porch. He got on top, but didn't do anything. He just lay there motionless, letting his weight rest on her.

"So, Cin, home for a while?"

"A couple of weeks. Why are you laying on me so heavy?"

"It's comfortable."

"Let me up."

"Why you left me like that?" he asked.

"I didn't leave you! I went away to school."

"You coulda took me with you."

"No, get off me!" She dug her nails into his arms but he pinned her hands.

"I'll get off, how come you didn't call when you got back?"

"I didn't want to, I was busy."

"Cut your hair too?" Frank asked and eased his weight off her slightly.

"Yeah. Now how am I gonna get back in the house?"

"Knock, ring the bell."

"You hopped out the window, hop back in, please Frank!"

"No, I don't think so. I like it like this. Just think how cold I am being on top. My ass is freezing."

Cindy, quiet, cried on Frank's neck. Then she sobbed loud once and couldn't stop. Frank stood up and dressed.

"I can't stand that. Look, I'll see you later." He finished dressing. He walked off the porch, and turned to see Cindy holding herself and crying loud enough for the neighbors to hear, and ringing the doorbell like she was trying to push her finger through it. The porch light came on. The door opened, Mrs. Jameson had a kitchen knife in her hand. Debra and Brenda were standing behind their mother and wouldn't move, so when Cindy tried to get into the house they blocked the way. Cindy held on to her mama. Frank squatted and watched for a moment, then walked toward the porch.

"Get off my lawn, Frank, or you gonna be stabbed and dead," Mrs. Jameson said.

Frank kept walking toward the porch. Mrs. Jameson backed into the house and threw the knife as she slammed the door.

When the police got there they found the knife, but no blood on it and no sign of Frank. Mrs. Jameson gave them a description, and the area of town where he lived. They told her to call them if he returned or if she saw him anywhere, but there was no need. Frank had pulled a permanent vanishing act.

Cast Out

IT WASN'T MIDNIGHT YET. Gumbo got his keys out and tried opening the front door as quietly as possible. Inside the house his parents' bedroom door was open, but they weren't in bed. He heard their voices from the kitchen. He thought about going back outside but didn't, instead he headed toward his bedroom. He stopped, they were talking about him again. He stood in the dining room and listened. They were both drunk.

"But Ba, he's been bad before."

"Uh-huh, they just about sent him to jail and he still won't mind no curfew."

"He minds, if you talk to the boy."

"What he needs to mind is an ass-whuppin'."

"He's too old for that."

"No, he's not."

Gumbo was sick of their conversation. He walked into the kitchen, his mama out of surprise shut up, but soon as she got used to him popping up out of nowhere, she worked herself into a finer state. Mr. Villabino tried to calm her but she wouldn't go for it.

"You big-headed hoodlum, you s.o.b.ing piece of shit coming in late when we told you."

Gumbo interrupted his mama, he pushed past her and said "Move! You some crazy-assed people talking like that about me, your son! That's some shit!"

After he shouted what he had to say, he started for his bedroom again, but his father was now blocking his way. Gumbo didn't slow, he pushed his father aside and walked out the kitchen. He shut and locked his bedroom door and turned on his radio. The grumbly shouts of his father still managed to get inside the room, but he thought his parents would leave and go to bed once they figured they couldn't get at him. He lay down on his bed and put his pillow over his head. A loud noise made him hop up. It sounded like somebody was beating the bedroom door with a bat or something. He opened the door and there his mama was, baseball bat in hand, ready to whack the door again. When she saw Gumbo she charged into the room swinging at him. Gumbo retreated, she was drunk and would hit him. His father ran in the room, he was carrying a golf club.

"Ba, don't hit the boy, Ba!"

Mrs. Villabino wasn't listening she was swinging hard at Gumbo's head. Gumbo ducked and knocked her with his shoulder into the open side of the sliding door closet. His father yelled and swung his golf club at Gumbo. Gumbo was surprised at the whizzing sound it made and how much it hurt smacking into his arm. His father dropped the golf club.

"Lord, I done hit the boy, Gumbo!"

Gumbo picked up the club up and broke it.

"Fucked up old drunks!" he yelled.

His father wouldn't look at him, he stared down at the floor. Then Gumbo heard his mama behind him. The back of his head tingled where he thought she was going to hit him. He ran out the room and out the house. He decided he was going to be a traveling man.

Social Work

THE EVENING ATTENDANT WALKED into the recreation room waving his arms to draw the attention of the guests of the Evercare sanitarium.

"It's nine o'clock, everybody to their rooms."

Gumbo watched the evening attendant shoo the small crowd of guests away from the TV, and move them toward their rooms. Most went quietly, but one lingered in the recreation room and the evening attendant hurried back for him. Arnold sat in front of the TV and ignored the evening attendant's orders. Finally, when the attendant looked mad enough to hit him, Arnold said something.

"I want to watch *Rockford Files*. I can do it, you know I can do it. I'm responsible, you know I am. I'll put myself up, you know I'll do it."

The evening attendant looked at Arnold sternly. "You'll put yourself up?"

Arnold nodded. "You know I will."

"Gumbo, you'll make sure?"

Watching, but not paying much attention, Gumbo said yeah without thinking about it. The attendant walked over to Gumbo to make sure he was being attentive.

"Lock up and if anything at all happens, call me. Don't do anything yourself."

Gumbo quickly went back to sweeping. Arnold made him nervous; he was one of the few people in the sanitarium that could talk and make sense. Gumbo went to his office for a break. He didn't like the job but he had to stick with it. He sat at his table, turned on the radio and put his head down for a nap. It wasn't a hard job, but most of the time he sat around in his office which was a big closet, and waited for the morning shift so he could go home. He didn't have much to do around the sanitarium. Just mopping and cleaning and stuff like that. Now and then, he'd have to go and check on the guests.

After a while, Gumbo got up from his table. He picked up his pail, went to the sink and filled it with hot water, put the sponge in, turned off his radio, and headed out to clean the walls and look in on the guests. He started cleaning the walls of a brightly lit hallway. He wasn't cleaning the portion of wall lower than his belly. He didn't get on his knees for the little money they were giving him. When he reached the first room he tried the handle to make sure the door was locked. It wasn't. He looked in, the room was empty. Arnold was still out. Gumbo knew where he was, Arnold liked to visit his girlfriend. Gumbo hurried over to her room. When he got there, he tried the door, and as he thought, it was locked. He knocked but nobody answered. He could hear people inside.

"Open up!" Gumbo shouted.

"Go away!" somebody answered.

"Open up or I'm gonna get my keys."

"Leave me alone. I'm with my girlfriend."

"Open the door!"

A few moments later, Gumbo heard the door being unlocked. When he opened the door, Arnold was in the bed, under the covers with his girlfriend. Gumbo went over to the bed to drag him out.

"No! I can't go."

"No?" Gumbo asked as he easily dragged the skinny man out of the bed. The covers fell off Arnold's girlfriend. She was a fat pale girl who looked like she was in her thirties. Arnold was normal as far as Gumbo knew. He didn't like to do him up.

"Don't take me! Please don't take me!" Arnold shouted.

"I gotta take you back. The day attendant is gonna be here soon."

"You know how it is. I don't cause trouble, but I need her! I need her real bad."

Gumbo put Arnold on his shoulder and carried him out of the room and pretty far down the hallway before he noticed Arnold's girlfriend was following them.

"Tell her to go back. You're gonna get the both of you in big trouble."

"No. We've got things to do."

"What things. You're gonna get your asses tranquilized."

"We have to slap bellies."

"Slap bellies? I know you, Arnold, you're not stupid. Anybody that reads as much as you do ain't stupid. I'm not going to lose this job. You're going in your room. When the day attendant comes, go visit her. Then you can slap bellies."

"No. We have to now."

Gumbo managed to carry Arnold to his room. He opened the door and pushed Arnold inside and locked it. Arnold banged on the door a few times and was quiet. Gumbo sighed, then remembered Arnold's girlfriend. He had to get her locked up too. He turned around and there she was, sitting on the floor naked. Gumbo took her hand and pulled her up.

"Come on now. Time to go back to your room."

He led her to the room. She didn't argue when he opened the door and led her in. He wondered if she could talk, he never heard her say anything. She lay on the bed and opened her legs and rubbed herself. She wasn't pretty, she was ugly. He didn't want to stay with her, but he couldn't leave the room. Watching her had him hypnotized. He walked toward her feeling like a zombie. He couldn't stop himself. He unzipped his pants and she reached out to touch him. Before very much time had passed, it was over. Arnold's girlfriend huddled herself in a ball and ignored him. Gumbo covered her with a blanket and left the room. He was queasy with guilt. He walked to Arnold's room and opened the door. Arnold was lying on his bed, looking up at the ceiling, smiling. Gumbo stood by the door and called to him.

"Your girlfriend wants you."

Arnold looked up at him. "Got a cigarette?"

"Arnold, go see her."

Arnold slid off the bed and hurried out the room. Gumbo got to the room in time to see Arnold going inside. He locked them in and went back to his office. He knew after the day attendant made his rounds he would be fired. But that was better than quitting. This way he could collect unemployment.

Visitor

IT WAS LATE EVENING by the time he arrived at home. He parked across the street from his house. As he was getting out of his tiny car, he turned in his seat to see Dinky grinning at him. He tried to be cool and not show he was startled.

"What's up, Dinky?"

"Nothing much, what you been up to?"

"Same old thing."

Dinky was always glad to catch Garvy when he came back into the city. Garvy liked to see Dinky too, when Dinky had something to say and wouldn't look at him like he had just sailed the seven seas or something.

"You just get back?"

"Yeah."

"Still up at Santa Barbara?"

Dinky was standing so close to the car door Garvy couldn't get out.

"Dinky, stand back a little."

Dinky stepped away and let Garvy out of the car. Garvy remembered he had some things in the trunk that he wanted to take into the house. But he decided to talk a while longer, the lock on his trunk was broken, so he thought it would be a good idea to wait till Dinky left before he opened it. He was looking at the trunk hood and the gnats that were crawling on top of it. He was wondering if he should have parked down the street and not under the street light.

"What's happening, Dink! Garv!" Onla said as he walked up.

"Nothing much," Garvy said. Dinky nodded his hello.

"Back in the city, huh Garv?"

"Yep." Onla had been away, too, he was skinny when he went in, now his arms were large, larger than Garvy's. Onla didn't have a shirt on, just a pair of tight, black pants. He had his arms crossed, and every now and then he would flex his arms.

"Look at his arms, Dink. Onla got big arms now."

Garvy was laughing as he talked. Onla uncrossed his arms, and crossed them back again.

"Still lifting weights?" Garvy asked.

"Naw, don't lift nothing but bitches," Onla said smiling.

"What you doing to stay so big?"

"Playing ball, shooting hoop all day."

"Where you're playing?"

"At UCLA."

"Yeah."

"All pros up there. Wilt and Kareem and Norm Nixon. I don't even try to drive, just shoot from the outside. Ain't getting myself hurt."

Garvy and Dinky watched Onla, who looked like he wanted to say something more about basketball.

"What you doing at Santa Barbara? Chasing them white girls?" Onla asked.

Garvy shrugged. He hadn't seen Onla in four months, and that was the first time he had seen him since he was released. He waited there, waiting for Onla and Dinky to leave so he could open his trunk. But it didn't seem as though they were leaving. He looked at Onla's arms and thought about how long it took him to get them that big...three years lifting weights in the place. Onla moved closer to him and showed him a cut on the back of his hand.

"It's not healing right." Onla said.

"Yeah," Garvy said. Dinky leaned over to see but Onla didn't seem interested in showing Dinky his sore.

"What you think, Garv?"

Garvy leaned closer.

"How you do it?"

"Tripped playing ball."

"Show it to my mama, she knows all about that stuff."

"Yeah, I'll come by later. Gonna go get something to eat."

Onla walked away from them in his usual hurry to be somewhere. Dinky wandered off, too, leaving Garvy alone. He waited for a bit, then took the stuff out of his trunk and went into the house.

jervey tervalon grew up in South Central Los Angeles.
He currently lives in Pasadena, California, and teaches writing
at the California State University at Los Angeles. His first novel,
Understand This, was published in 1994.

INCOMMUNICADO PRESS

BOOKS

Steve Abee KING PLANET 146 pages, $12.

Dave Alvin ANY ROUGH TIMES ARE NOW BEHIND YOU 164 pages, $12.

Dave Alvin THE CRAZY ONES 156 pages, $12.

Elisabeth A. Belile POLISHING THE BAYONET 150 pages, $12.

Iris Berry TWO BLOCKS EAST OF VINE 108 pages, $11.

Beth Borrus FAST DIVORCE BANKRUPTCY 142 pages, $12.

Pleasant Gehman PRINCESS OF HOLLYWOOD 152 pages, $12.

Pleasant Gehman SEÑORITA SIN 110 pages, $11.

Barry Graham BEFORE 200 pages, $13.

R. Cole Heinowitz DAILY CHIMERA 124 pages, $12.

Hell On Wheels Edited by **Greg Jacobs**, 148 pages, $15.

Jimmy Jazz THE SUB 108 pages, $11.

Michael Madsen BURNING IN PARADISE 160 pages, $14.

Peter Plate ONE FOOT OFF THE GUTTER 200 pages, $13.

Peter Plate SNITCH FACTORY 182 pages, $13.

Scream When You Burn Edited by **Rob Cohen**, 250 pages, $14.

The Spacewürm I LISTEN 160 pages, $13.

Jervey Tervalon LIVING FOR THE CITY 185 pages, $13.

Unnatural Disasters Edited by **Nicole Panter**, 256 pages, $15.

We Rock, So You Don't Have To Ed. by **Scott Becker**, 261 pages, $15.

Incommunicado also releases spoken word CDs and distributes select CDs from New Alliance Records and Ruby Throat Productions. See our website for audio clips and the full list.

Available at bookstores nationally or order direct: Incommunicado P.O. Box 99090 San Diego CA 92169 USA. Inside the U.S., include $3 shipping for 1 or 2 items, add $1 for each additional item. Outside the U.S., $7 shipping for 1 or 2 items, add $2 for each additional. For credit card orders call 619-234-9400. E-mail: severelit@aol.com. For online ordering, book excerpts and audio/video clips, go to the website: http://www.onecity.com/incom/
Distributed to the trade by Consortium Book Sales and Distribution.
Please help us destroy American Publishing. Thank you.